"Please unlo[ck...

Marc was standi[ng...] bathroom, plea[ding...] out so he could apologize.

"How could you have brought a client home like that without even letting me know?" she argued through the closed door.

"How was I to know you'd chosen this particular night to greet me in your underwear?"

"I wanted it to be a surprise," Hannah wailed. "I wanted it to be a romantic, exciting, passionate night. Instead, it turned out to be the most embarrassing moment of my life!"

"Come on, Hannah, Bloomenthal thought I was damn lucky to have a wife like you."

"You don't have a wife like me. He only thinks you do. I'm not really a *wife* at all. I'm a total failure."

"Oh Hannah, you've never failed at anything. We can still have fun, excitement, passion. Please unlock the door. . . ."

To Valerie and Bret

———— 🍎 ————

ELISE TITLE
is also the author
of these novels in
Temptation

LOVE LETTERS
BABY, IT'S YOU!
MACNAMARA AND HALL
TOO MANY HUSBANDS

Making It

ELISE TITLE

MILLS & BOON LIMITED
ETON HOUSE, 18-24 PARADISE ROAD
RICHMOND, SURREY TW9 1SR

First published in Great Britain in 1991 by Mills & Boon Limited, Eton House, 18-24 Paradise Road, Richmond, Surrey TW9 1SR

© Elise Title 1991

ISBN 0 263 77528 3

21 – 9110

Made and printed in Great Britain

I was married once. It was the result of a misunderstanding between myself and a young woman.

Oscar Wilde
The Importance of Being Earnest

Prologue

Get Me to the Hall on Time

HANNAH LOGAN'S ALARM clock went off at 6:30 a.m. Tossing her dark unruly hair away from her face, she reluctantly rolled over onto her back. She leaned to her right, switched the clock from jarring alarm to soft classical music and automatically reached for her well-worn appointment book on the bedside table. Her name was gold embossed in the center of the black leather cover, and at the bottom left-hand corner, in smaller lettering, was her company's name and address, also embossed:

UNICOM CONSULTANTS, INC.
243 West 86th Street
New York, N.Y. 10122

Hannah flipped to the day's tabbed page—December twelfth. Despite knowing the schedule by heart, she slowly, reflexively read down the page.

7:15 bkfst meet/ Hobson—bring McCallister portfolio

8:40 unit meet/ concept planning for the Wal-
ston development

10:00 Neilson/ organizational dynamics—focus
on fast-growth ventures

11:45 hairdresser—wash/trim

12:15 lunch meet/ Petit Maison/ Harrington—

Hannah slipped the pen from the inside binder of the book and jotted down next to Harrington: *Confirm that Lois reserved non-smoking.*

She paused again at the next entry—2:15 City Hall.

Fully awake now, she sat up in bed, pen poised, her breathing coming a little quicker, the tip of her tongue unconsciously sliding across her lower lip; 2:15 City Hall, she read again. Then, after a moment, she scribbled next to the entry: *Marc.* She started to write Welles, then laughing to herself, she stopped, finishing the *W* with *Wedding.* Hannah's heather-green eyes blinked several times as she focused on the word *Wedding.* A little shiver of anticipation zigzagged down her spine. "Wedding," she said aloud, and then after a moment, switched all the letters to capitals. WEDDING. She went over the letters several times so that it was impossible to see that the word had originally been written in lower case.

She fell back against her pillows, her eyes still focused on her WEDDING entry, forgetting that if she didn't get up in another minute, grab a quick shower and get dressed, she'd be late for her 7:15 breakfast meeting. The tip of her tongue darted back out as she wrote in, beside WEDDING: *Don't forget the Rolex.* As if she ever would forget.

Forcing her eyes downward, she scanned the rest of her busy day's schedule: 3:45 Unicom/ board meeting. Yes, she thought, she'd make it from City Hall in time. The actual ceremony only took ten minutes. A few minutes to gather afterward for hugs and kisses, a few minutes alone with Marc to savor the moment, then she'd have time to grab a cab and make it uptown, maybe even getting a minute or two to compose herself before the meeting got underway. After all, it wasn't every day a girl got married.

Hannah scanned the rest of the page. The reception at her mother's was penned in for 8:30. She knew her mother would like her to get there early, but Hannah hadn't offered any promises. She hoped the board meeting would end by 6:30, but chances were it could run to seven. After the meeting, she still had some last-minute work to tidy up in her office, then get to the cleaners to pick up her dress, change and make it all the way down to Grammercy Park for the reception. She'd be lucky if she got there on time, much less early.

Slowly Hannah shut the appointment book, her eyelids fluttering closed, her heart beating rapidly as she thought about this, her wedding day. She'd waited a long time for the right man to come along, a man who both loved her and fully supported her career. She and Marc had it all figured out—a perfect merger of love and work. And they were starting off on the right foot. Hannah sighed, a thrill of excitement spreading through her. She felt so full of faith in herself, in Marc, so confident, unafraid and unapprehensive about their future together. She was sure they were going to make it.

MARC WELLES SLIPPED his Give It All You Got T-shirt over his broad shoulders as his day's schedule came up on the computer monitor in his den. Tucking the shirt in his black nylon running shorts, he gave the screen a quick study.

Across the top of the monitor was printed, Daily Log—Marc Welles—December 12

> 6:15 Meet Lou Fischer at the gym for squash.
> 7:45 Kelly's Deli—breakfast meeting with Hampton
> 9:00 Chase Manhattan Bank—financing start-ups for Morgan project
> 10:15 office—finish up figures on the Fieldmar Magni-Viewer
> 11:15 meeting with Colloti re: creative financing package
> 1:30 grab a hot dog at Zekes, haircut at Mike's, get blue suit from cleaners
> 2:15 City Hall

Marc's gray eyes lingered on the entry, then he leaned over and typed in Ring next to City Hall.

His fingers still resting on the keyboard, he gazed at the entry quite wistfully, not a usual expression for the supposedly unsentimental, hard-driving Marc Welles, VP at Center for Strategy Research, one of the top marketing research companies in the country. Truth be known, Marc did have a sentimental side, but he'd long learned sentiment and business didn't mix. He had a reputation for being quick, cool-headed but decidedly strong and confident. No, sentimentality was not a key to success in the fast-track corporate world Marc Welles smoothly moved about in.

Brushing aside sentiment and an assortment of other emotions he decided were best not to identify, he let his eyes move down to the next entry in his schedule. A three o'clock meeting with Mel Templer at Jacar Communications. Jacar was both uptown and across town from City Hall. It wouldn't give him much time for more than a brief wedding kiss before he took off. Still, he reminded himself in typical pragmatic and sincere fashion, he and Hannah would have the rest of their lives together. Like Hannah, this was his first marriage and he meant it to be his last.

Finishing his check on the rest of the day's schedule, his only concern was a 6:15 p.m. meeting over in Jersey City. He knew he could cut the meeting short, but still, getting across the Washington Bridge and over to Mary Logan's Grammercy Park apartment by 8:30 wasn't going to be any easy feat. Well, he'd do his best. If he was a few minutes late he was sure Hannah would understand. Knowing Hannah, she'd probably be scrambling to make the reception on time herself.

1

The Wedding Reception

452 Grammercy Park

THE WEDDING RECEPTION was being held at the apartment of the mother of the bride, Mary Logan. In the large, high-ceilinged living room, a buffet table draped in white linen tablecloths stretched for twelve feet in front of a bank of floor-to-ceiling windows. The curtains were open to the view of snow-covered Grammercy Park below. Beyond the park, the dark night sparkled with city lights like diamonds against velvet.

The living room was a large, comfortable space that could easily accommodate the fifty-odd invited guests. Contemporary artwork studded the cream-colored walls, a thick Oriental rug covered a large square of the wood parquet floor and the furnishings, an eclectic mix of modern and antique, had been especially arranged in small groupings for the occasion. Overhead, a large crystal chandelier cast a warm yellow glow over the festivities.

Diane Quinn, Laura Winninghoff and Pamela Adams gathered together in practiced cocktail poses off to one corner of the room. The three women, all young, bright, attractive colleagues of Hannah's at Unicom, sipped demurely from crystal champagne flutes.

"Lucky gal, our Hannah," Laura said, finishing her drink and glancing around for the good-looking dark-haired waiter who was cruising the room with a tray of refills.

Diane's expression was pensive. "Marc is a catch. There's no denying that."

Pam raised a brow. "But?"

Diane, a lanky redhead, toyed with the lacy collar of her blue-and-gray print silk dress. "It's just that they've moved kind of fast into this marriage bit."

Laura giggled. "Moved fast? Why, haven't you heard? According to our Hannah, Marc isn't even giving up his apartment."

Pam, Hannah's closest friend as well as colleague, quickly came to the bride's defense. "Hannah explained all that. Her apartment is too small for them and his is too far downtown. It just wouldn't be practical. They've been looking for a more suitable place ever since they decided to tie the knot, but you know how long it takes to find a decent apartment in Manhattan."

"Who knows," Diane said philosophically. "Maybe the marriage will have more of a chance if they don't find that decent apartment too fast."

Laura grinned. "Yeah, they can always stay in touch at the press of a button."

"Oh, right," Diane said with a laugh. "They did exchange those gold-plated cellular phones for their engagement. Instant communication anytime, any place."

"Don't laugh. Maybe if Don and I had invested in cellular phones we'd still be living happily ever after,"

Laura said quite earnestly. "We just never seemed to have any time to talk seriously about anything."

"I still say," said Diane, her smile more of a smirk, "that it's absolutely impossible for two people engrossed in their careers to make it in a marriage. My philosophy is live together while the going is good, and get out when the going gets rough. Keep things light, casual, and stay uninvolved."

Pam scowled. "Why must we all be so damn cynical in this town when one of our own finds the man of her dreams and chooses to get married?"

"Have you checked out the divorce figures lately?" Laura asked.

Diane grinned at Laura. "Some of which you contributed to yourself."

Laura sighed. "Well, I gave it my best shot."

"It's going to work for Hannah and Marc," Pam said with stubborn insistence. "I think they're the perfect couple."

Laura, still looking to spot the dark-haired fellow with the champagne refills, commented, "Speaking of the perfect couple, where are the happy bride and groom? It's almost time to cut the cake, isn't it?"

THE CHEF REACHED ACROSS the buffet table and handed plates with poached salmon and tiny new potatoes sprinkled with dill to Harris Porter and John Moss, fellow market researchers at Marc's firm.

"So what odds do you give 'em?" Porter asked Moss as they made their way to the salads.

"I'm a bad one to ask, considering my own divorce just became final a few weeks ago."

Porter nodded. "Personally, I wouldn't do it. Too risky. Work is complicated enough. Who needs more complications? A guy can give just so much, right?" He helped himself to endive and radicchio.

John Moss took garden spinach and marinated artichoke hearts. "Then again, there's no denying Hannah Logan is something special. Smart, articulate, successful and a knockout to boot. And according to Marc, the two of them are going into this thing with their eyes wide open."

Harris Porter gave his colleague a sly wink. "Yeah, right. Let's see how their eyes look after the honeymoon wears off."

HARRIET AND GEORGE LOGAN, Hannah's aunt and uncle, made themselves comfortable on the gray-and-pink striped velvet sofa, exchanged smiles with other guests milling about and then turned to each other with rueful looks.

"What was the rush? That's what I asked my sister," George Logan said to his wife.

"And what did Mary say?"

"She said, 'You're an accountant, George. You figure it out.'"

Harriet gave her husband a distressed look. "What does that mean?"

"It means," he said with exaggerated patience, "that by marrying before the New Year, there are certain significant tax advantages—"

"George!" Harriet's distress turned to alarm. "You can't mean to say that Hannah got married simply because it was . . . cost-effective?"

George raised his thick gray brows. "Me? I didn't say anything. You want the lowdown, you ask my sister."

Harriet sighed. "It's all so...unromantic. I know your sister wanted Hannah to have a big church wedding. I must say I admire Mary for taking this all so well. I know I wouldn't be so understanding if our Margie told me she was squeezing her wedding in during the afternoon recess of her kindergarten class."

George wore a reminiscent smile, taking his wife's hand in his. "Remember our wedding, Harriet. You were such a beautiful bride."

Harriet smiled wistfully. "I offered my wedding gown to Hannah if she wanted to borrow it."

George chuckled wryly. "Can you just see her wearing satin and lace to City Hall?"

"Talking about seeing her, where is the bride?" Harriet asked. "Or the groom, for that matter."

Unicorn—243 West 86th Street

HANNAH WAS IN A FRENZY. The meeting had run past seven-thirty and she'd had to send Lois, her secretary, to pick up her dress from the cleaners while she finished up the pile of paperwork on her desk. The work had to be done since she'd be gone for the next three days.

Her honeymoon. Three days in St. Croix. Three whole days and nights with Marc under a tropical sun, away from the grime, slush and hassles of Manhattan. Three sun-filled, romantic days and starlit nights. It was going to be wonderful. Why, she and Marc hadn't spent three whole days and nights together since . . .

Hannah frowned. In the fourteen months she'd been dating Marc, they'd never actually spent three whole days and nights together. Their work schedules were both crazy and they could never manage to get away for any extended period. But they'd managed a reasonable break this time. If ever there was an occasion for an extended holiday, Hannah mused, this was it.

This is it. This is it. This is it... The words kept playing over and over in her head. *This is it.* Not just the honeymoon, the three whole days and nights together. This was it. A whole life together. A commitment to love, honor... respect and cherish each other "'til death us do part." Not as her friends would say, "'til divorce us do part."

Hannah was experiencing the first tiny quiver of insight into the impact of her marriage, a momentary blotting out of the brightness, of the certainty of making it. She felt an unfamiliar nudge of anxiety. Doubt? Self-doubt had never been part of Hannah Logan's agenda.

Her green eyes, lightened by the glow from her computer monitor, shifted to the silver-framed photo of Marc on her desk. She lifted her fingers from the keys, clasped them together and placed them on top of a huge pile of folders as she stared at the photo of the blond-haired, smiling man. He was very handsome. The photo captured Marc's angular, chiseled features, his clear gray eyes, his thick, wind-strewn hair. But as good as it was, the picture didn't do him justice. In real life, his handsome face radiated something more than good looks. There was confidence, humor and an undercurrent of sensuality that lit up his eyes, colored his voice.

She gave her new husband's photo a radiant smile. "I love you very much, Marc," she whispered.

Yet that echoing phrase—*this is it, this is it*—kept droning in her head like an irritating refrain of a song you never much cared for in the first place. *This is it, this is it, this is it...* She'd actually gone and gotten married today to a man she'd never even spent a whole three days in a row with.

A new refrain popped into her head. *I just hope we've done the right thing.* The new refrain mingled with *this is it,* making up an altogether disquieting and tuneless little ditty.

Hannah stared long and hard at the steady, confident gaze in Marc's eyes that shone from the photo. Slowly the jarring chorus faded from her mind, then dissolved altogether. Her head cleared. Thinking of Marc's confidence revitalized her own. What a silly fool she was being. She'd found the perfect husband. Marc believed she'd be the perfect wife. So that made them a perfect match. They'd anticipated all the pitfalls; they were alert to all the hazard signs. And they knew, together, they could avoid them. Of course, they'd done the right thing.

Lois, her hard-working executive secretary, breathless and more than a little frazzled, came rushing into the office with Hannah's dress wrapped in plastic.

"Sorry it took so long. I couldn't get a cab over there. Then they couldn't find your dress at the cleaners." The trim, middle-aged woman checked her watch. "Oh, no, it's almost nine. Weren't you supposed to be at your party by eight-thirty? Oh, if only that stupid clerk—"

"Relax Lois, I'm just finishing up here anyway. I wouldn't have been able to get out any earlier." Hannah made one final entry, saved her file and powered down her computer. "There," she said with finality. "Done."

Lois ripped off the plastic wrap from the dress as Hannah rose from her chair, unzipped and stepped out of her simple gray shift. After Lois handed over the cranberry voile dress, she stood by Hannah's desk and glanced over at Marc's photo. She'd only been working for Hannah a couple of months and had never actually seen Marc in person.

"Nice-looking, isn't he?" Lois said, her nearsightedness making her bend a little closer to the photo.

"Yes. Very." Hannah, standing in her white silk chemise, slipped the cocktail dress over her shoulders.

"He looks like a good solid type."

"Yes. Very."

"You must be very happy."

"Yes. Very."

Lois smiled as she watched her tall, slender boss struggle to put her wild mane of ebony hair into a reasonable chignon. "You've got the jitters, right?"

Hannah gave up on her hair and let it tumble pell-mell over her shoulders as she gave her secretary a wan smile. "Yes. A little," she admitted with reluctant honesty.

"Natural enough."

"It is?"

"It was for me twenty-seven years ago."

"Twenty-seven years," Hannah echoed, her voice tinged with a mix of wonder and admiration. "You've been married for twenty-seven years?"

Lois laughed awkwardly. "Well . . . no. We got married twenty-seven years ago, but actually it only lasted more like twenty-seven months. If that."

"Oh, that's a shame," Hannah muttered with more sympathy than seemed warranted.

"It was a big mistake," Lois said, shaking her head. "I hardly knew him. Boy, did I learn a lot about him after the wedding, though. Unfortunately, most of what I learned I didn't much like. We just saw most things differently. I wanted kids, he didn't. He wanted his mother visiting every Sunday for dinner, I didn't. I bought him a puppy for his birthday and he told me he hated dogs." Lois stopped abruptly. "Sorry. I didn't mean to get carried away." She gave Hannah an encouraging smile. "I'm sure you and your new husband will live happily ever after. Two such smart, successful people. I really wish you the best."

Hannah's second attempt at the chignon was worse than her first. Finally she gave up and simply brushed out her hair and pulled it back with a rhinestone-studded barrette.

Smoothing back the loose strands she'd failed to capture in the clasp, Hannah said firmly, "Well, I've known Marc for more than a year. I don't think there are likely to be too many surprises for either of us."

She tried hard to sound confident about her observation, but her confidence, much to Hannah's surprise and horror, was abandoning her. Her mind was racing. *Maybe we don't really know each other all that well,* she was thinking. *Yes, we've been dating for over a year, but how much total time have we actually spent together?* Her mouth set in a firm line. *But it was quality time,* she told herself. *We have talked. We've communicated...a lot. But...but for all I know, Marc could be allergic to dogs. I...I don't think he knows I've got a thing against cats. No allergy. Just never liked them. Big deal. I'll tell him. Anyway, with our busy life-styles we'd certainly never consider taking on a pet.*

Hannah caught Lois watching her closely and she felt a tinge of paranoia. Could Lois read her mind?

Tossing her head back, she smoothed down her dress and gave Lois a level look. "I guess there are some things Marc and I haven't actually had a chance to talk about, but . . . but we both feel communication is important. Why, we even exchanged cellular phones so that we can talk whenever we want. Even if it's just to touch base and say hi."

"Well, isn't that a nice idea?" Lois said pleasantly.

What Hannah didn't admit to her secretary was that, if truth be told, most often a "hi" was all they had time for. Still, that would improve now that they were married. Or at least, once they got truly settled.

A yellow taxicab on the Washington Bridge

MARC WELLES CHECKED his new Rolex for the twentieth time. Eight-fifty p.m. A thin bead of sweat broke out across his brow.

"It's long past rush hour. I don't get it. What's the holdup?" he asked the cabbie. It hadn't been the first time he'd asked the question. They'd been inching through traffic for the past forty-five minutes and had come to a full stop in the middle of the bridge about ten minutes ago.

"Like I said before, it must be an accident or some construction. It should clear up." The cabbie glanced into his rearview mirror. "Late for a hot date?"

Marc managed a weary smile. "Something like that. I'm late for my wedding reception."

The cabbie did a double take. "Wedding reception? Where's the bride? Got tired of her already and left her in Jersey?" he bantered.

Marc wasn't in a joking mood. "We got married at City Hall in Manhattan this afternoon and the reception's on Grammercy Park. I was supposed to be there by 8:30."

"Uh-oh, that's not a good way to start off the marriage, friend. If I'd showed up late for my wedding reception, my wife would've handed me the ring and my head on one of the caterer's silver platters."

Marc did laugh now. "Oh, it's not Hannah that worries me. It's her mother and the rest of the family. They were none too pleased that we didn't have a big church wedding and one of those huge gala receptions at some flashy restaurant afterward. But neither Hannah's schedule nor mine would allow it. Besides, we both wanted to keep this as simple as possible."

The cabbie chuckled, inching the taxi a few feet forward. "Hey, whoever it was clued you in that marriage was simple, sure gave you the wrong clue. Both of you work, huh?"

"Why...yes, we've both got very demanding careers. Hannah—my...wife—is a consultant on urban planning. She's only been with her firm for a couple of years but she's really gone far. She's bright, innovative, really impassioned about her work."

The cabbie nodded. Marc only saw the back of his head, missing the wry grin on his face. "And let me guess. You're a hotshot lawyer."

"No. I'm in market research."

"I bet you're good."

Marc shrugged. "I'm doing okay. I plan to do better."

"Ambitious, huh?"

"What's wrong with that?" Marc was frustrated by the traffic tie-up and irritated by the distinct hint of irony in the cabbie's tone. He was also annoyed at having forgotten to stick his cellular phone in his briefcase when he'd left the office. It wasn't at all like him to be forgetful like that, and he refused to admit he might have been more than a little rattled over the reality of his wedding when he'd raced back to his office from City Hall that afternoon.

The cabbie persisted with the line of talk. "And the new wife, she got ambitions for you, too?"

Marc chose the distraction of conversation rather than contemplating his inner turmoil. "My wife and I happen to both be ambitious people. But we also happen to be very sensitive to each other's feelings. We don't try to compete with each other, we're both secure, we plan to share all household responsibilities...we both have a...a very positive view of marriage."

Typically a private man, Marc found himself quite atypically compelled to ramble on. "We're not cynical like most of our friends when it comes to marriage. Sure, we've read all the statistics. We know how tough it is for a career couple to find the time and energy to be together. And maybe we won't be able to spend as much time together as we'd like because of our professions. But what time we do spend is going to be quality time.

"Oh, sure, we could have opted for less risk, just moved in together like plenty of our friends. We considered all of our options, evaluated them, considered the downside risks and the benefits—financial, emotional, and let's face it, medical. In these times, it makes sense to stick with one safe partner."

"Yeah," the cabbie said, a wide smirk on his face as he inched the taxi forward a few more inches. "Sounds like you covered all the bases. Guess you can figure it'll be clear sailing ahead."

452 Grammercy Park

MARY LOGAN, THE MOTHER of the bride, corralled her daughter in the foyer as Hannah breathlessly entered the house. "Do you realize what time it is?" Mary scolded, raising a maternal but imperious finger at her. "Your own wedding reception, you're hours late and Marc isn't even here yet. I'm absolutely mortified."

Hannah, used to her mother's bouts with mortification, took off her coat and gave her mother a bright kiss on the cheek. "I'm only forty-five minutes late and it wasn't my fault. The cleaners couldn't find my dress."

Mary Logan was used to her daughter's excuses. "A likely story. Anyway I spoke with your secretary at nine and she said you'd just finished up your work and were on your way. Really Hannah, there's a time and place for work...."

Hannah put an affectionate arm around her mother who, at five foot five, was a good three inches shorter than her. "Hey, for a frantic mother of the bride, you look pretty good, Mrs. Logan." She gave her mother's teal-blue silk cocktail dress an approving nod. "Great color. You should wear it more often."

Mary Logan was also used to her daughter's attempts at distraction. "Really, Hannah, I don't understand you. Or Marc. Why you couldn't have had a normal, civilized wedding..."

"It was very civilized, mother. It was certainly 'civil,'" she teased.

"My only daughter. Do you know how many years I fantasized about a big church wedding for you? I could just picture you walking down the church aisle in an exquisite white satin gown and veil...."

"It's a busy time for both of us. We just wanted something simple and quick."

"Quick is right. You and Marc racing into the judge's chambers, saying a couple of breathless 'I do's' and then practically leaving skid marks on the floor of the City Hall lobby as you raced out for separate cabs. Why, before I could throw the rice, you two were nowhere in sight. It would have landed all over some poor fellow coming to pay a traffic fine."

Hannah laughed and gave her mother a big squeeze. "I do adore you." She started for the living room to greet her guests, but her mother took a firm grip of her arm, holding her back.

"Hannah, you do love Marc?"

"What a question, Mother. Of course I do. And Marc loves me. Just because we believe in being practical and refuse to become overly sentimental about a wedding ceremony doesn't mean we don't intend to give everything we've got to this marriage. Oh, I suppose it's hard for you to understand, but Marc and I have a very clear concept of how we want to model our marriage. We see it as . . . as a limited partnership, in a sense."

Mary Logan sighed. "A limited partnership? Darling, there is nothing limited about a good marriage."

"Look, Mother, in a limited business partnership there are clear-cut and definite controls that work to your advantage, as opposed to an unlimited partnership. You don't tie up all your assets, you keep separate projects going, you provide a sense of organization, you minimize risk. . . ."

"Oh, Hannah, Hannah, you sound like you've taken your marriage oath on the *Wall Street Journal* instead of a bible."

Hannah frowned. "Really, Mother, I wish you'd have a little more faith in me and Marc."

"Which reminds me. Where is Marc?"

Hannah wasn't about to admit it to her mother, but she was wondering the same thing. She'd expected him to be here already. She certainly wished he were. The edginess that had begun back in her office had followed her here like a shadow.

"I'm sure he's either been held up by his meeting in Jersey or got stuck in traffic." Hannah could hear the note of irritation in her voice and it surprised her. She was usually very understanding, as was Marc, about unintended tardiness. It was all part of the package that came with having high-powered careers. But now, Hannah found herself feeling uncharacteristically annoyed. Then again, this was their wedding night.

2

The Wedding Night

Midnight at the Plaza bar

"WE REALLY SHOULD get going and let our two love-birds head up to their honeymoon suite," Pam said, addressing the small group that had decided to follow Hannah and Marc to the hotel for a last wedding toast . . . or two.

John chuckled. "What's the hurry? They're going to have the rest of their lives to honeymoon."

Harris Porter, looking more than a bit pie-eyed, took up his glass. "One more toast. Here's to Hannah and Marc. May their honeymoon last at least as long as..." He paused, spilling some of his champagne. "What's the record for honeymoons, anyway?"

"Mine lasted for six months," Laura offered.

"Yeah, so did your marriage," Diane said with a snicker.

Laura giggled. "That's true. Boy, when the honeymoon's over, it's really over. So, enjoy it while you can, you two."

With an abruptness that drew everyone's attention, Hannah sprang out of her chair. "I've . . . I've got to go to the . . . powder room."

Marc leapt up, too. "Sure, Hannah."

"By myself."

Everyone laughed. Only then was Marc aware he was standing. Flushing, he sat back down.

As Hannah hurried off, Diane leaned closer to Harris Porter. "Wedding night nerves," she murmured sotto voce.

Marc could feel a bead of sweat start to break out across his brow, and he quickly wiped it away. *Never let 'em see you sweat.* Why was he sweating, anyway? he wondered. The wedding night. Big deal. It wasn't as if this was going to be the first time he and Hannah'd be making love, after all. Just the first time making love as a married couple. *A married couple.* He could feel a new sweat working its way through his pores.

"What's the matter, old buddy?" Harris asked jocularly. "Not nervous, are ya?"

Marc forced a quick, confident smile. "Just eager," he said glibly.

"Uh-oh, he's giving us signals," John announced. "Can't wait to get that beautiful bride of his in a compromising position."

Pam gave John a disapproving look. "Let's not let envy make us crass."

Laura sighed, reaching across for Marc's hand. "You and Hannah are so lucky. You're just the ideal couple, that's all there is to it," she declared.

"And just what is it that makes them the ideal couple in your eyes?" Diane simpered sarcastically.

Laura frowned. "Really, Diane, I think it's obvious. They're on the exact same wavelength. They know just what they want. And they know how to get it."

"Every couple seems ideal at first," John commented reflectively. "I mean, I think Liz and I were the perfect couple. Why, I can remember plenty of people telling us that. They told us that for years. The crazy thing is, when Liz and I broke up, you know what everyone said to me? They said they knew it wouldn't work and they'd been expecting us to split for years. Go figure. I'm still trying to understand what went wrong."

"I thought Liz told you that what was wrong was you never cried," Harris said.

"Don, my ex, never cried," Laura mused. "But, I don't actually think that ever bothered me. But maybe it did, and I just didn't know. Or maybe I was crying so much, I never gave him the chance. Now that I think about it, I wonder if that was part of why our marriage broke up. Then again, I'm not sure I could have coped with Don crying. Not that I think it's a sign of weakness or anything—"

"Personally," Diane broke in, "I think men can turn it on just as easily as women. And if it's turned on, it's simply pure manipulation."

"I don't agree one bit," Pam stated. "I think every woman wants a man who's capable of deep emotion, a man who's willing to show his feelings openly."

"Crap," Harris declared, slapping Marc on the back. Champagne splashed over the goblet Marc was navigating toward his mouth. "You tell 'em if you don't agree with me. When it gets right down to the nitty-gritty a woman still wants a dry-eyed man who runs the show."

A round of boos came from the women.

"You don't agree with that, do you, Marc?" Pam demanded.

"Well...no. I mean...I think..." Marc stopped. What did he think? He was having trouble getting his thoughts straight. Too much bubbly. He blotted champagne stains from his trousers, forgetting the question.

"Be honest now, Marc, have you ever blubbered in front of Hannah?" John asked earnestly. "I personally think Liz's expectations were unrealistic. I don't think very many men go around blubbering. Do you, Marc?"

Before he could answer, Pam broke in. "I know for a fact Marc has shed a few tears in front of Hannah."

Marc spilled some more of his champagne, on his shirt this time. He was aghast. He certainly never took Hannah for the sort who'd go around telling her friends intimate details, especially about him. Besides, he couldn't remember ever having cried in front of Hannah. That made his brand new wife a liar as well as a gossip.

Pam grinned, observing the groom's reddened complexion. "Relax, Marc. It was no big deal. It was when you and Hannah went to see that French film last month. I can't even remember the name. But Hannah raved about it. And she happened to mention that you both were sniffing back tears at the end."

"Oh, that doesn't count," Diane declared.

"Well, I don't know," Laura mused. "It does show Marc's got a sentimental side."

John laughed. "Yeah. Left side or right side?"

"Backside," Harris said with a chuckle.

"That's disgusting," Laura snapped. "Come on, Marc. Don't you think you have a sentimental side?"

Marc smiled uncomfortably. "Well, I think...I think Hannah's been in the powder room a long time."

"You've gotta give that new wife of yours a little breathing space," Harris quipped. "You know how they're always beefing about needing space."

"Marc knows all about needing space," Diane interjected. "He's not even moving into Hannah's apartment."

"That's the way, old buddy," Harris said approvingly. "Now if every wife let her husband have his own pad, there'd be a lot less divorces. Just think, you won't have someone complaining all the time about how you don't stick your dirty clothes in the hamper, or nagging you about remembering to put the cap on the toothpaste...."

"I don't know why women never seem to have a problem capping the toothpaste and yet I've never met a man who seems able to do it," Diane mused. "Must be genetic."

"Do you put the cap on the toothpaste, Marc?" Pam inquired.

"Really," Marc said, frowning, "hasn't Hannah been gone a...longish time. Maybe she's sick or something."

"She did look a little white when she took off," Laura reflected.

"I'll go check," Pam said, rising.

"HANNAH?" Pam saw the one closed stall in the otherwise empty powder room. "Hannah, are you in there?"

"Mmmm."

"Are you okay?"

"Mmmm."

"Marc's getting antsy. He's worried you might be sick. You aren't feeling sick, are you?"

"Uh-uh."

"Nerves?"

"Uh-uh."

"Cramps?"

"Uh-uh."

"Well then . . . what's wrong?"

There was no reply. Pam frowned. "Listen, Hannah, every bride's a little jittery on her wedding night. It's perfectly understandable. It's not so much the *wedding night* part, as it is the realization that you've actually gone and done it. Gotten married, I mean. It's a big step. And let's face it. A lot of people trip over it and fall flat on their faces."

A faint moan came from the stall.

"Not that you and Marc will have any worries about that. We were all just saying out there how you and Marc are the perfect couple. You're both so . . . together. You've thought it all out so cleverly. You're both so reasonable and understanding. You both have a very clear sense of yourselves and each other."

A faint sniffling sound was Hannah's only response.

"Hannah?"

"Mmm?"

"Are you crying?"

"Uh-uh."

"Is there some reason you're not coming out of that stall?"

She mumbled, "I'd just . . . rather not."

"Can you tell me why?" Pam asked, baffled by her friend's utterly uncharacteristic behavior.

"No. Not really."

"What should I tell Marc?"

"Could you tell him . . ." Hannah paused. "I'd like to see him . . . for a minute."

Pam blinked. "In here?"

"Yes, please."

PAM GAVE A QUICK CHECK then smiled awkwardly at Marc. "All clear. She's . . . uh . . . in the last stall."

Marc stepped nervously inside the powder room, sticking close to the door.

"Hannah?"

"Marc? Is that you?"

He grinned. "How many men who drop into ladies' powder rooms know your name? How many men drop into powder rooms, for that matter?"

"I suppose . . . not too many."

"Hannah, couldn't we talk someplace less . . . gender related?"

"Marc?"

"Yes, Hannah?"

"Are you . . . fond of dogs, Marc?"

"Am I fond of dogs?"

"Do you like dogs?"

"I don't understand, Hannah."

"It's not a very difficult question, Marc."

"No. I mean, yes. I like dogs...all right. I don't spend much time thinking about dogs, Hannah. Is there some particular reason you're thinking about dogs on this . . . particular night?"

"No. No particular reason, really."

Marc crossed the powder room and lightly rapped on the closed door of the stall. "Hannah, please come out."

"I feel . . . really stupid, Marc."

"Don't feel stupid, Hannah. You're very smart."

"They must all be having quite a chuckle back at the table."

"No, they're not." He wiped his brow. "It doesn't matter. All brides get . . . emotional."

"How do you know? How many brides have you seen lock themselves in bathrooms?"

Marc smiled. "Now that I think about it, not too many."

"Not any."

"So, you're different. You're special. Come out, Hannah. Please. Before some woman walks in and sees me and I end up spending our wedding night in the clink charged with indecent loitering."

"I don't know what's wrong with me. This is so . . . dumb. I just feel . . ."

"I know," Marc said softly. "So do I."

The latch clicked. The door opened. A pale, anxious Hannah stood staring at her new husband. "Oh, Marc, you do?"

"I do, darling."

Hannah hugged him and then smoothed back her hair. "I must look dreadful."

"You look beautiful."

Hannah smiled, but then she gave Marc an appraising look. "You don't look so good."

"I . . . don't?" He frowned. "I feel . . . okay. I feel fine. Maybe just a little . . . off. Too much champagne. Every time I set my glass down, Harris filled it up again." He swayed a little.

"You're pale. And you're sweating." Hannah's voice was concerned.

Marc smiled crookedly. "I think I do feel a little . . . odd. A little . . . queasy."

"Here, sit down," Hannah said, squeezing past Marc and guiding him to the toilet seat. "I'll get you some wet toweling." She hurried across to the bank of sinks and started pulling paper towels from the dispenser. "That Harris. I truly think the man has a drinking problem and he isn't happy unless everyone around him gets drunk, too." She turned on the cold water tap and ran her finger under the water until it was cold enough. Then she soaked the towels, squeezed them out and flattened them into a compress. When she turned around, the stall door was closed.

"Marc? Are you all right?"

Just as she was calling out his name, the door to the powder room opened.

A well-dressed middle-aged woman stepped in and gave Hannah a curious look. Hannah smiled awkwardly. "My friend. She's . . . sick. Too much champagne."

As Hannah was talking, Marc was throwing up, so he had no idea the woman had come into the powder room.

"Oh, Hannah, I'm so embarrassed," he moaned from inside the closed stall. "I just want you to know one thing."

Hannah's eyes shot to the woman fixing her makeup at the sink. The woman was staring sharply at Hannah in the mirror.

Hannah patted her chest. "Bad cold. Laryngitis."

"Hannah?" Marc called out tentatively.

"That's all right...hon, you can tell me...later. You just...stay put...and sit quietly in there...for a while."

"I love you, Hannah."

The woman at the sink stuffed her makeup bag back in her pocketbook, spun around and gave Hannah a glare of disgust. Hannah responded with a wilted smile.

Just as the woman was exiting in a huff, Marc was saying, "Let's go up to our room, darling, and climb into bed...."

UP IN THE MAUVE-AND-CREAM parlor of their lavish suite, they quickly decided to forgo the complimentary, celebratory magnum of champagne courtesy of the management. Both of them had had more than enough to drink and neither of them had much tolerance for excess. Hannah and Marc prided themselves on being levelheaded, reasonable, take-charge people. It was hard to have any of those qualities now, with their heads pounding and their stomachs still rumbling.

"Are you feeling better?" Hannah asked solicitously.

"Oh yes. And you?"

"Much. Much better." Hannah sounded earnest, but there was a distinct lack of conviction in her voice.

"Then the issue of ... dogs ... isn't an issue now?"

She gave him a quirky smile. "No. It isn't an issue."

"Good." Marc sat down on the delicate mahogany Hepplewhite settee. He pressed his palms together, stretched, then rose. "Well . . . this is nice . . . isn't it?"

"The suite? Oh, yes. Great. Beautiful."

"It was nice of your mother. . .arranging this for us."

Hannah laughed. "Mother loves the Plaza. Besides, she thinks we ought to observe some conventions. She wasn't exactly thrilled with the wedding ceremony. Her only child and a daughter at that. I guess she feels I've deprived her of a . . . special moment."

"Yeah, my family wasn't too thrilled, either," Marc admitted. "And, of course, Dad couldn't get away on such quick notice."

"Your mother could have come."

"No. She never goes anywhere without my dad. It's always been that way. Besides, she's terrified of flying. And the rest of the family, well, Susie just had the twins, and Gordon travels, and Alicia . . . well, she's got the three kids and besides, she gets overwhelmed by Manhattan. Thinks she's going to get mugged walking off the plane."

Hannah laughed. "Well, there is that possibility."

"Talking about planes, you did pick up the tickets yesterday?"

"For St. Croix? Of course." Hannah sighed. "Just think, tomorrow night we'll be sitting out on our own private patio overlooking a glistening aquamarine ocean, stars filling the sky, a warm tropical breeze ruffling our hair."

"Sounds wonderful."

"Everyone says St. Croix is the perfect spot for a honeymoon. Three whole days. Three whole days and nights together. Just think about it, Marc."

"I am."

Hannah detected an odd note in his voice. "You aren't sorry I chose St. Croix?"

"No. No. St. Croix is…great. Three whole days and nights…"

"I was thinking earlier… we never really spent that much time together."

"Sure we have." He frowned. "Haven't we?"

"No. I was thinking about it and…no, not three days and nights in a row."

Marc gave an awkward little laugh. "Well, I think for our very first three days and nights together in a row, there's no better spot than St. Croix."

"John Moss mentioned he went to St. Croix on his honeymoon," Hannah mused. "Or was it Bermuda?"

"Bermuda," Marc said firmly, not that he really remembered. He just didn't want to associate the honeymoon of his now-divorced friend with his and Hannah's.

"Bermuda's nice. But I don't think it's really warm in Bermuda this time of year." Hannah didn't particularly want to connect with the divorced couple, either.

"No. St. Croix will be much better," Marc said.

"It's too bad we couldn't get away for a longer stretch," Hannah murmured. "But three days… and nights, well, that's still…great."

"Sun and fun. Three days of it. Just think." Marc tried to inject a note of enthusiasm in his voice, but at the moment, he was secretly wondering how he was going to cope with a honeymoon if he was having so much difficulty coping with the wedding night.

"And nights," Hannah murmured, ambling over to the large arched window overlooking Central Park and drawing back the heavy brocade curtain. "It's starting to snow. I hope there won't be any problems getting out of Kennedy tomorrow. It would be awful if our plane was grounded."

Marc sat down on the settee again. "I...uh...forgot to mention...that I need to stop by at the office...before we take off tomorrow. Just a few...loose ends to tie up. It shouldn't take me more than a couple of hours."

"Oh, no problem, darling," Hannah said, turning from the window to face him. "It'll give me time to do some paperwork at home. That way I won't have to take any work with me."

"Oh, that's good. I won't either. Take any work with me."

Hannah smiled. "This is a busy time for both of us."

"Right."

"Mother wondered if she ought to contact some realtors while we were gone."

"Why?"

"To...uh...keep an eye open for an apartment. For us."

"Oh, right. Sure. Sure, that would be great."

"I think she thinks our arrangement is...a little...weird. You know, each of us keeping our separate apartments."

"It's not...like that. I mean...it's just during the week."

"And just until we find a suitable place for . . . both of us."

"Right. I'm not worried," Marc stated firmly.

Hannah's face brightened, but her fingers were clutching the brocade drape. "Neither am I. I'm not the least bit worried."

Marc rose from the settee and pressed his hands together again. "So . . ."

"So . . ." Hannah echoed.

Slowly, Marc stretched out his hands toward her. "Come here, Hannah."

She hesitated. "Meet me . . . halfway."

He smiled. "Always. I'll always meet you halfway."

But neither of them took a step.

"Marc?"

"Are you going to ask me about dogs again, darling?"

She smiled. "No. Not about dogs."

"Ask me anything you want, Hannah."

It took her a few moments. "Marc, we are going to make it, aren't we? I mean . . . what happened to John Moss and to Laura Winninghoff . . . it won't happen to us, will it?"

"No," Marc answered emphatically. "Never, Hannah. You're nothing like Laura."

"What do you mean?"

"It's just that . . . she's so unrealistic, so flighty. She has all these romanticized notions about marriage. I mean . . . not that marriage shouldn't be romantic . . ."

"Oh, I know you don't mean that, Marc. And you're right, I'm nothing like Laura. And . . . and you're nothing like John Moss." She giggled. "Thank goodness."

There was a slight twitch at the corner of Marc's mouth. "What do you mean?"

"Marc, really. John Moss is so ... uptight. He's so ... stiff and ... come on, Marc, you're nothing like him."

"Hannah?"

She could hear clear portent in the way he said her name, and she experienced a spurt of alarm.

"Do you ... ?" He paused. "How do you feel ... ?"

"Yes? How do I feel ... ?"

"Remember that French film we saw a couple of months ago?"

Hannah smoothed back her hair. "Which one? We've seen several French films."

"The one where the woman died at the end. And her lover was trying desperately to get through traffic to be with her."

"Oh, yes. I remember. That was a great movie. Didn't you think it was a great movie?"

"Yes. Oh, yes. Great. The thing is ... well, you kind of ... teased me afterward."

"I did?" Hannah tried to think back. "What did I tease you about?"

"You said my eyes were red. From crying. Because the ending was sad."

"Oh ... right. I didn't mean to tease you, Marc. My eyes were red, too. It was a really sad movie. We were both crying at the end. No big deal."

Marc let out a breath. "Exactly. No big deal."

"Have you been angry at me all these months for having teased you?" Hannah asked with concern.

"No. No, of course not. I just was thinking earlier this evening about . . . men who cry. . . at movies."

"I think it's nice that you cry at movies, Marc."

"I don't do it very often, Hannah."

"Well, that's okay, too. Neither do I."

"What I'm saying is, I don't want you to think I'm overly. . . sentimental. But, on the other hand," he was quick to add, "I don't want you to think I'm—"

"I don't," Hannah said softly. "I think you're . . . just the way I want you to be."

"Hannah, that's exactly how I feel about you."

They walked toward each other, matching step for step until they were practically nose to nose.

"This feels . . . a little silly," Hannah admitted. "I mean . . . it's so formal."

"It's the . . . wedding night." Marc smiled softly, taking hold of her hands. "There are all of these . . . expectations."

"Right. Expectations. What we need to do is...relax. Treat this night like any other night we just happen to spend in a posh suite at the Plaza."

Marc gave her shoulders a little friendly squeeze, trying for a casual air, which didn't quite materialize. "We don't have to make love tonight...if you don't want to, Hannah. I mean...we've got our whole lives ahead of us."

"Oh, I want to." She hesitated. "Of course, if you're not up to it . . ."

"Oh, I'm up to it."

"I mean . . . your stomach."

"My stomach? Oh, that's fine now." His face reddened, thinking about that episode in the stall of the powder room. "I must say, this is definitely a day of firsts. My first wedding, my first visit to a ladies' powder room . . ."

Hannah started to giggle. "You should have seen that poor woman's face when she heard you say, 'I love you.'"

He laughed. "A girlfriend with laryngitis. Well, if she'd known the truth, she'd probably have called the cops and I really might have ended up spending my wedding night behind bars."

Hannah kissed Marc lightly on the lips. "I'm glad you didn't end up in the clink. My wedding night just wouldn't be the same without you," she said with a teasing smile.

Marc stroked her cheek with the back of his hand. "I do love you, Hannah."

They kissed, but somehow neither of them could shake the feeling that this night of required bliss had an orchestrated air about it.

"Maybe we should . . . go into the bedroom," Marc suggested.

"Yes. Yes, that's a good idea."

Marc took a deep breath. Then, catching Hannah off guard, he swept her up into his arms à la Rhett Butler.

Hannah circled Marc's neck with her arms and leaned her head to his shoulder. In truth, it wasn't so much a romantic gesture as it was a need to rest her pounding temples. She'd been trying to will away her headache for the past hour to no avail.

Unbeknown to her, Marc had been surreptitiously popping antacid tablets into his mouth during the same hour. They weren't having much effect. Halfway to the bedroom, he stopped.

"Hannah?"

"Yes, Marc?"

"What would you say to a...little walk? I...always love . . . walking in the snow."

"You do? I didn't know that." Hannah frowned. How many other things about Marc didn't she know. *Cheer up*, she told herself. She did know he liked dogs. Not that she was keen on having a dog.

"So, what do you say?"

"To a walk? Oh, fine. Great."

"Great. A walk in the fresh air, with the snow glistening . . ."

"Maybe you should put me down first," Hannah suggested.

Marc grinned. "I don't think I've ever held you in my arms like this, Hannah."

"Another first."

He kissed her lightly on the lips and set her down.

On the way out the door, Marc popped another antacid tablet and Hannah prayed that the crisp night air would cure her headache.

3

We've Only Just Begun

Hannah's apartment—4354 West 97th Street

"THANKS FOR HELPING ME pack, Pam. I don't know why I'm so discombobulated today," Hannah muttered as she searched her bureau drawer for the bra top to her black bikini.

Pam grinned. "I'd be pretty discombobulated myself *the morning after*. Was it . . . wonderful, Hannah?"

"Mmmm," Hannah mumbled awkwardly.

"Gosh, a suite at the Plaza. The perfect spot for a wedding night."

Hannah slammed the drawer shut. "Perfect," she muttered.

"Did you get any sleep at all?"

"No," Hannah admitted, "not much." What she was too embarrassed to admit to Pam was that her lack of sleep had a lot more to do with anxiety and a headache that just wouldn't quit than it did passion. Then there was the matter of Marc's overdosing on antacid tablets. Not that they hadn't made love. They'd managed it somehow. Oh yes. Where there's a will, there's a way. However, whoever made up that little adage failed to point out that sometimes the way wasn't always all that satisfying.

Hannah ducked her head into her closet where she kept a cardboard box packed with some of her summer things. She thought that possibly the missing top to her bikini might be there. Shorts, jerseys and cotton nighties went flying in her search. Finally, exasperated, Hannah sat back on her heels. "It's gone. I've been robbed. The bikini bra burglar has struck again."

Pam chuckled. "Do you think the bra burglar is any relation to the sock burglar? And while we're on the subject, why does the sock burglar always steal just one sock in a pair, never a matched set?"

"For the same perverse reason the bra burglar takes the top of the bikini but leaves the bottom. He wants to keep us, his victims, in a constant state of frustration and hopelessness."

"Wow, Hannah. Don't you think that's taking too bleak a position? I mean, a missing sock or a missing bra shouldn't really make you feel hopeless."

Hannah sat down fully on the floor, bending her legs and hugging her knees against her chest. "I suppose I could buy a new bikini down in St. Croix."

"Or you could go topless," Pam suggested airily, waiting for a snappy rejoinder. Few women were more modest than Hannah.

"I suppose," Hannah muttered.

Pam gave Hannah a bemused look and then joined her on the floor. "Hey, married life has changed you already."

"Huh?" Hannah gave Pam a blank look.

"You, topless?"

"What are you talking about?"

"Hannah, I just said you could go topless down on St. Croix, and you said, I suppose."

"Oh, is that what you said?"

"What's wrong, Hannah? I thought after you and Marc had your little chat in the powder room last night, everything was great between you two."

"It was great. It is great. It's just...being married isn't exactly what I expected."

"What did you expect?" Pam asked.

"I expected...it would be...pretty much the same." Hannah picked up a pair of white shorts she'd tossed from the closet and absently folded them. "I didn't think I'd feel so...strange and awkward. You say 'I do,' two little words, and all of a sudden it's a whole new ball game. I'm up there in this decadently posh suite at the Plaza with a man I've known intimately for over a year now and suddenly...I feel weird. And he feels weird. And...it's just not the same."

"But it isn't supposed to be the same, Hannah. Marriage is supposed to be different. That's the point. It's like Dr. Rusman says. Living together isn't enough for a successful union. Only in marriage can two people truly exchange the promise of commitment."

Hannah got up and placed the white shorts she'd folded into her suitcase. "Who's Dr. Rusman?"

Pam looked shocked. "Who's Dr. Rusman? Dr. Harold S. Rusman just happens to be one of the world's leading experts on marriage. His book, *Commitment: The Ties That Bind; The Ties That Chafe*, has been at the top of every bestseller list in the country for the last two months. The book is positively brilliant. Rusman conceived the intimacy/loneliness dichotomy. See, it's a paradox. We're all afraid of intimacy, but at the same time we're terrified of loneliness. Rusman makes some very cogent points. Like he points out that loneliness is something we can accomplish by ourselves, whereas commitment is something we have to do together."

Hannah stared to giggle.

"Really, Hannah, I don't see what's so funny." Pam frowned. "Maybe I didn't say it right."

Hannah, suddenly feeling better than she had in days, came over and gave her friend a big hug. "Thanks, Pam."

"For what?"

"Oh...just for being up to date on the bestsellers out there, for knowing Dr. Horace S. Rusman..."

"Harold. And I don't know him, Hannah. Not personally. Although I have to say when I read his book I actually felt like the man was talking directly to me." She gave Hannah a thoughtful look. "Maybe you should pick up a copy at the airport. If you want my opinion, I think it's must reading for every married couple who wants to maximize their relationship. It would give you and Marc a broader perspective. Of course, you'll never get Marc to read it. Men never do. But you could highlight the salient points for him. Rusman's got this wonderful section on sex—'the gift that goes on giving'...."

A burst of laughter broke from Hannah's lips. "'The gift...that goes...on giving'?" Hannah started laughing so hard tears began running down her face.

"Go on and laugh, Hannah, but Rusman's got your number. I think you'd especially find his last chapter very enlightening."

Hannah tried to swallow back the laughter. "What's his last chapter? Money—the gift that goes on spending?"

"It's on taking the marriage vows," Pam said archly. "He calls it, 'I Do. Do I?'"

Hannah stopped laughing.

Center For Strategy Research—32nd and Madison

"I DIDN'T EXPECT to see you here today, Welles."

Marc looked up from his desk and gave a frazzled nod to Douglas Ryder, the trim, energetic, inspiring thirty-six-year-old head of CSR. "I'm always here on Saturdays, Mr. Ryder."

"I know that, Welles, but aren't you taking off for Bermuda today on your honeymoon?"

"St. Croix. Yes. I'm meeting Hannah at the airport." Marc checked his watch. "I've got a couple of hours though, so I thought I'd just finish up a few things. Especially as I won't be back until Wednesday."

"Too bad about the timing of the Bloomenthal package, or you could have had the whole week."

"That's okay. Hannah has to be back on Wednesday anyway. She's consulting on the city's new lower West-side park project."

Ryder gave one of his bright smiles of approval. "Good choice, marrying a career woman, Welles. They know how the game's played. They start off on the right foot, knowing there just aren't enough hours in the day to get everything done. I remember how my first wife, Betsy, used to constantly nag me about never spending enough time with her. She puttered around the house all day getting bored, and then I was supposed to rush home and amuse her. Now, a career wife, especially one looking to get ahead, hasn't got time to be amused. She's got her own schedule, her own responsibilities. She's savvy to the demands that have to be met in order to get ahead."

Marc nodded, a thoughtful expression on his face. "Oh, absolutely. If anything, Hannah's schedule is even busier than mine at times."

Ryder leaned forward, resting an elbow on Marc's desk. "I'll give you one piece of advice, though, about being married to a career woman. My second wife, Cindy, was a lawyer. A regular dynamo. Man, you wouldn't ever want a face-off with that woman in court. The problem was, she didn't know when to quit. She was always trying to show me how slick she was, how tough, how shrewd, how she didn't really need me. Okay, she wouldn't take my name when we tied the knot. No big deal. I'm all for women's lib. She didn't want to cook for me, clean for me . . . no problem, we hired a housekeeper. But, man, when she got her partnership and started bringing in bigger bucks, did she ever lord it over me. Now she wasn't my equal, she was better than me." Ryder wagged a finger. "The point is, Welles, you've got a career woman, you've got to always keep the competitive edge. That's the key to a successful marriage, Welles."

Marc smiled faintly. If Ryder knew the key to a successful marriage, he mused, how come he was a three-time loser? Ryder'd just gotten divorced again, this time from Angela, a schoolteacher.

Ryder straightened up and gave Marc's desk a light rap. "You better keep your eye on the weather, Welles. Snow's picking up. Give yourself a couple more minutes getting to the airport." He started off, but then stopped and turned back around. "Since you still have some time, though, how about just giving that Bloomenthal account one last scan. I had Matheson give it a peek yesterday and he did raise a couple of questions. Shouldn't take you more than thirty, forty minutes to address them." Ryder smiled slyly. "You do good on this one, Welles, and you won't have any worries about keeping the competitive edge."

"No problem," Marc said, trying his best to sound sincere. But there was a problem. No way was it going to take only thirty, forty minutes to address Matheson's questions. Two, three hours was more like it. Well, maybe he could cut it down to an hour and a half and still make it to the airport on time.

Kennedy Airport

HANNAH ACTUALLY ARRIVED at the airport a good forty minutes ahead of schedule, despite the snow. She checked in her luggage and strolled over to the gift shop to pick up some chewing gum for the flight. While she was waiting in the checkout line, her gaze fell on the rack of paperback books near the register. There on the top shelf, above a sticker marked #1, was a picture of the famous Dr. Harold S. Rusman himself. Across his gleaming bald pate was the word, *Commitment*. And there, under his goateed chin, was the rest of the title, *The Ties That Bind; The Ties That Chafe*.

Hannah studied the cover and smiled to herself. Personally, she'd never been one for self-help books. It was her opinion that too many women wasted too much of their valuable time analyzing and dissecting relationships. Her smile deepened as she thought about her Uncle George's summation of a successful relationship. It was a line he quoted from Woody Allen. "Eighty percent of success is showing up." As for the other twenty percent . . . Uncle George offered that it helped to show up with a smile. And if you showed up late, with flowers.

Hannah did her best to affect a casual air of indifference as she took the self-help book off the shelf. She told herself she'd just skim the table of contents for a little chuckle.

"I vouldn't vaste my money," a voice behind her remarked in a Germanic accent.

Hannah's cheeks reddened as she looked over her shoulder at a petite late-middle-aged woman with short, tidy gray hair who reminded her immediately of the sex therapist, Dr. Ruth. "Oh, I wasn't . . . going to buy it." She quickly put the book back on the shelf. "I was just . . . waiting to buy my gum." She held up the package as proof.

The diminutive woman smiled pleasantly. "I've been married thirty-seven years and I vouldn't give two cents for vat they tell you in books."

"Oh, I couldn't agree more," Hannah was quick to say. And then more slowly, "Thirty-seven years? To the same man?"

"Sure, the same man."

"Oh, that's so nice," Hannah gushed.

"Nice? Sometimes it's nice. Sometimes...not so nice. Sometimes dull, sometimes not so dull. Sometimes you want to bake him a lemon meringue pie, sometimes you want to throw the lemon meringue pie in his face." The little woman chuckled. "My Harry loves lemon meringue pies. You understand what I'm saying?"

Hannah gnawed at her lower lip. "Marriage has its ups and downs?"

"Exactly."

"But some marriages have more ups, and some have more . . . downs."

The little gray-haired lady glanced at the wedding ring on Hannah's finger. "So what about you? More ups or more downs?"

"Well, I've actually only been married . . . a short while. Actually, I've only been a wife for one day."

"Uh, a newlywed? And already you're looking at books for answers?"

"I wasn't—"

"You want some advice about marriage? I'll tell you just vat I told my daughter, Marilyn, on her vedding day less than a year ago. It's very simple. You get married, you stay married. If you marry a lemon, learn how to make lemonade from lemon juice." She gave Hannah a little nudge. "A cup of sugar can go a long way."

Hannah was tempted to ask the loquacious woman if her husband was a lemon, but she knew that would be rude. Besides, it was her turn at the register.

"So, married one day," the woman reflected as Hannah extracted a bill from her wallet. "You must be going on your honeymoon."

"Yes. St. Croix in—" Hannah took her change and glanced at her watch "—twenty-five minutes."

"Oh, nice. Very nice." The woman craned her neck around. "So, vere's the lucky husband?"

"He's on his way. He's probably checking in his bags this very minute." Hannah put the loose change in her pocket. "Where are you going?"

"Me? No, I'm vaiting for my daughter. She's flying in from Chicago." The woman paid for her roll of mints and followed Hannah out of the shop. "She's been a mess since the divorce."

"Marilyn?"

The woman nodded. "Do children ever listen to their mothers?"

CSR offices—3:30 p.m.

MARC BALANCED THE PHONE between his neck and shoulder as he jotted down some notes in the margin of the Bloomenthal spreadsheet. Finally, the Musak clicked off and a live voice came on the line. "Hi," Marc said quickly. "Can you please tell me, when's the next flight to St. Croix?"

There was a lengthy pause before the voice replied, "There's one leaving in twenty minutes on Northeast, sir."

"No, I can't make that one. When's your next flight?"

"Well, there's a—"

"Oh, could you hold on just a second?" Marc put his hand over the mouthpiece of the phone as Doug Ryder came up behind him.

"Everything under control here, Welles?"

"Just finishing up."

Ryder gave his shoulder a squeeze. "I knew it wouldn't be a problem for you."

"Right. No problem," Marc replied dryly as Ryder breezed out of the office. "Sorry," he said into the mouthpiece. "When is the next flight after the three-forty to St. Croix?"

There was no response.

"Oh great." He dialed again.

Back at Kennedy

IT WAS LESS THAN twenty minutes to takeoff when Hannah heard the loudspeaker message.

"Will Hannah Logan please come to the information counter at Northeast Airlines?"

Hannah felt a jolt of alarm. Marc. Oh no. Something had happened to Marc. An accident. A car crash. Wait. He didn't have a car. A taxi. A taxi colliding with a bus. Bodies strewn everywhere. Marc's body... A widow even before the honeymoon.

As Hannah raced to the information counter, she cursed her lousy wedding night. She should have tried harder; she should have taken aspirin earlier; she should have been sexier. Even a little more relaxed would have made a difference. *Oh, Marc, Marc, I love you. Just be alive. That's all I care about. Anything but widowhood I can cope with....*

"Hello ..." Hannah pressed one hand against her pounding heart and clutched the telephone receiver with the other.

"Hannah?"

"Marc? Marc, it's you. It's you. Oh, Marc, thank God." Tears of relief rolled down Hannah's face.

"I'm so glad I caught you in time, Hannah. I was afraid you'd already boarded."

"Oh, Marc, Marc, I love you. I love you, Marc. Did I even tell you I loved you last night?"

"I love you, too, Hannah. Look, I'm sorry about this."

"It's all right, darling. You're alive. That's all that counts. That's all that matters to me."

"I knew you'd understand. You see it's this damn Bloomenthal mess."

"Marc, Marc..." Suddenly Hannah stopped, her brow furrowing. "Bloomenthal? Who's Bloomenthal?" Bloomenthal, she thought, had better be the name of the injured taxi driver. But somehow, even before Marc responded, Hannah knew he wasn't.

"Ryder threw Bloomenthal at me before he ducked out of here. You see, he gave the workup to that bastard, Matheson, yesterday...I've told you about Matheson. Nobody nitpicks like Matheson. Well, he did have a couple of legitimate questions."

"Marc?"

"Yes, Hannah?"

"You're not in the emergency ward of a hospital, are you?"

"What?"

"No, I didn't think you were."

"Listen, Hannah, you catch that plane to St. Croix, slip into a sexy bikini and start working on your tan and I'll catch the next flight out. There's one at seven-fifteen tonight. We'll have a late supper on our patio—"

"You want me to go to St. Croix without you?"

"I've got another hour, two at the most, and I can wrap this up. You know how important this Bloomenthal account is."

"Right. Right, I know."

"That's my girl. Ryder said I was a lucky bastard to marry a woman who had her own career and knew all about deadlines. You're terrific, Hannah. Don't think I don't know how lucky I am. I don't need Ryder or anyone else to tell me."

"I'll wait here at the airport for you."

"That's crazy. Why sit in some dank, dreary airport when you could be sunning on white sands in the tropics? And when I do get there tonight, Hannah, we'll . . . really start our marriage. You know what I mean?"

"Oh, Marc, it just seems weird for me to fly off on our honeymoon by myself."

"I've got to go, Hannah. I want to finish here before Ryder shows up again with something else for me to do. Bye, darling. See ya later."

"Marc? Marc?" But he'd already hung up.

Coral Reef Hotel, St. Croix

"HELLO, MOTHER."

"Hannah?"

"You only have one child, Mother."

"Where are you, Hannah?"

"I'm in St. Croix. On my honeymoon."

"Pardon my surprise, darling, but not too many daughters call their mothers while they're on their honeymoon."

"Not too many daughters go on their honeymoons by themselves either, I bet."

"By yourself...? What are you saying? Where's Marc?"

"Where's Marc? I imagine he's with Bloomenthal. In spirit anyway."

"Hannah, have you been drinking?"

"Well...yes. A little. You see, since I am in the honeymoon suite, the management has been thoughtful enough to provide champagne and a large bowl of fresh fruit. I'm saving the fruit for the morning. It's a wonderful hotel. Really, I plan to recommend it to all my friends for their honeymoons. I'll say one thing. If you've got to be alone on your honeymoon, St. Croix's the place to be."

"Did you and Marc have a fight?"

"A fight? Oh, no. Marc and I don't fight. We've never had a fight. It's all in the way you approach things. And Marc and I approach disagreements and such in a very calm, reasonable fashion. And when two calm, reasonable people are...both calm and reasonable, there's no need for either of the parties of either part to lose their tempers."

"I don't understand you, Hannah. Truly, I don't. Your husband lets you go on your honeymoon alone. He's off with this Bloomenthal, whoever he is.... He is a *he*, isn't he?"

Hannah giggled. "Mother, really. Even a womanizing husband would at least wait until after the honeymoon to . . . to . . . Oh, Mother . . ."

"Hannah, are you crying, darling? Please don't cry, sweetheart. I'll leave the house this very minute and go find that husband of yours and put him on the very next plane to St. Croix."

Hannah sniffled back tears. "You can't."

"Why can't I?"

Hannah gave up trying to fight the tears. "Because Kennedy is . . . snowed . . . in. All . . . planes . . . are . . . grounded," she wailed. "Marc just . . . called . . . to tell me."

"Oh, no. Oh, poor baby. Don't cry. It's not so bad. By tomorrow . . ."

"Tomorrow? We only have three days. Had three. If Marc gets here tomorrow we'll only have two days left."

"Oh, but they'll be glorious days."

"Mother?"

"Yes, dear?"

"Is it still . . . snowing in New York?"

Mary Logan hesitated. "Well . . . a little."

"How little?"

"By tomorrow morning, I'm sure the airport will be open again."

"What if it isn't? What if I end up spending my . . . my whole honeymoon by myself?"

"Oh, I'm sure that won't happen, darling. Marc will get there."

"Mother?"

"Yes, darling?"

"Did you and Daddy have a . . . wonderful honeymoon?"

"Why . . . yes. Yes, we did."

"You went to Venice, didn't you?"

"Yes. Venice in the spring. It was the most romantic and beautiful spot in the world. We swore we'd go back again sometime. . . ."

"Was Dad a lemon?"

"What?"

"Oh, never mind. What counts is that Marc isn't a lemon. He's a . . . a peach. A peach of a guy . . ."

"I think it might be wise if you recorked that champagne and left it for another day."

Hannah hiccupped. "I wonder what Dr. Rusman would say about this?"

"Who's Dr. Rusman?"

"Oh, Mother, everyone, simply everyone knows the great Dr. Horace S. Rusman. Maybe if Marilyn had listened to him instead of her mother she might still be married right now. I mean, really, I doubt the ability to make lemonade ever prevented a divorce."

"Hannah, you're not making any sense. Please go to bed and get some sleep, darling. You'll feel better in the morning."

"I can't sleep in this bed by myself. It just . . . doesn't seem right to sleep in this huge king-size honeymooners' bed all alone. It's got . . . satin sheets."

"Well then, why don't you see if there's another room available for tonight? Tomorrow, when Marc arrives, the two of you can return to the suite."

"Oh, Mother, what wonderful advice. Just . . . just wonderful advice. I'm going to do just that. See. Sometimes children do take their mothers' advice."

A single room at the Coral Reef Hotel

HANNAH INCORPORATED the faint scratching sound into her dream. It was a strange dream filled with sailboats, jet planes, shadowy people darting in and out of dark alleys calling in low husky voices, *Bloomenthal. Bloomenthal. Wherefore art thou, Bloomenthal?*

"Hannah."

A new voice, louder than the others, was calling her name now. In her dream, Hannah warily addressed the bald-headed man with the goatee. *Is that you, Bloomenthal? What did you do with my husband?*

"Hannah, darling . . ."

If you're a man, Bloomenthal, you better prove it or forever hold your peace. . . .

"It's me, Hannah."

She felt him shaking her. *Get your hands off me, Bloomenthal. I'm warning you. . . .*

"Oh, Hannah, you look so beautiful."

You asked for it, Bloomenthal. This one's for Marc. . . . This one's for me. . . .

Somehow, the loud sharp grunt of pain broke through her nightmarish sleep. The sound, she realized with a start, was real. Here. In this room.

And then, as she bolted upright and saw the shadowy bent figure at the side of her bed, she let out a terrified scream, certain a maniac had broken into her room to molest her. She grabbed the lamp from the bedside table and was about to swing it at her attacker when his hand sprang out and grabbed the lamp from her.

She screamed again, certain he was about to swing the lamp at her.

Instead, he switched it on.

Hannah blinked and then her mouth dropped open. "Marc . . . ?"

Despite the pain in his gut from Hannah's two sharp jabs to his solar plexus, Hannah's new husband managed a faint smile. "Did you really think I'd desert you on our one and only honeymoon?"

"Oh, Marc. I. . . I thought. . . this was going to be the worst honeymoon in recorded history."

He bent over and kissed her, a long, passionate, hungry kiss. And then, before it ended, he scooped her up in his arms.

"What are you doing?" she gasped.

"Taking you up to the honeymoon suite," he murmured against her ear.

"But . . . but . . . I'm not dressed. I'm just wearing a . . . flimsy nightie."

"I can't wait." He dipped a little so she could grab for her negligee which she clasped against her body. Marc smiled, a sensuous, irresistible smile as he carried her up to their suite. And Hannah knew that the honeymoon had truly begun. . . .

4

An Almost Perfect Honeymoon

The first night

"TELL ME AGAIN," Hannah whispered, nuzzling closer to Marc. "Tell me how you managed to get here to me."

"Let's see." His hand was on her thigh. "I trudged over to 48th and Seventh Avenue to rent the car." His fingers did a delightful little *trudge* up her thigh.

"Mmmm." Hannah sighed, her hands stroking Marc's chest, marveling at his firm, strong body. "And then?"

"And then I drove through the snow to Philly." He let his fingers do the *driving.*

"Oh, yes . . . Philly. Oh, yes," Hannah moaned, her body arching up to meet his tantalizing strokes. "And . . . then?"

Marc bent his head, his tongue licking her lips. "And then—" his tongue slipped between her lips for a moment, his hands moving round to cup her buttocks and draw her closer to him "—I took a plane to Miami. . . ." He kissed her deeply on the mouth, and then his mouth and his hands began caressing her body with lustful abandon.

"Mmmm. I love . . . the Miami . . . part," Hannah moaned, marveling at Marc's ability to be so imaginative, creative and inventive a lover. She never would have guessed. Oh, he had been tender and eager to please in his lovemaking before the honeymoon. He'd been dependable, reliable, earnest, good and sweet. But their lovemaking was decidedly different now. Marc was different. And Hannah found herself being swept up in his uninhibited ardor.

"The Miami part isn't the best part," Marc murmured, clasping her wrists and drawing her arms high over her head, pinning them there. "The flight from Miami to St. Croix's even better." With his tongue, he traced a path downward from her breast to the center of her rib cage and then lower still, his strokes as delicate as a flower on her skin, and yet as deliberate as a bomber pilot who knew precisely where to strike for greatest effect.

His tongue thrust deep into her, and Hannah cried out, parting her legs, opening herself to Marc. Her muscles were expanding and contracting of their own accord, as if she were giving birth to passion.

Her body was like clay and Marc was molding it, shaping it, fitting it to him, first turning her frontward then backward. He moved on top of her and then they rolled so wildly, they landed on the floor, their fall cushioned by the soft, thick emerald pile carpeting.

Flushed, out of breath, perspiring, Hannah soared through the skies with Marc, touching stars along the way, capturing moonbeams. Her body had never before felt in such perfect physical and psychic sympathy with Marc, her love, her husband. Oh, yes, being married was different. Wonderfully, exhilaratingly different. Being married released unimagined depths of passion in them both. She'd had no idea how grand it was going to be. She laughed in the face of all the lousy statistics; she laughed at Dr. Harold S. Rusman's ties that chafe; she laughed at all the warnings and well-meaning advice given by family and friends, and most of all, she laughed at her own doubts and fears.

"Oh, Marc, this is wonderful," she whispered. "This is the way it's always going to be."

"No," he whispered back, swinging his body over her again. "It's going to get even better."

"Mmmm. Yes. Tell me again how you risked life and limb to get here. Start from the beginning."

"There was a snowstorm. And Kennedy was closed. But the airport in Philadelphia hadn't been shut down. So, I decided to rent a car. I trudged over to 48th and Seventh . . ."

For a while Marc kept talking and whispering and demonstrating how he'd found his way to her despite the obstacles. Hannah's breath came in irregular gasps as she drank in his words, absorbed his caresses, opened fully to him once again, thinking how it would always be like this.

The second day

THEY WERE LYING under a pastel-colored sky on a white sandy beach, while the waves of the blue Caribbean rolled into shore. "You should put on a little more sun block, Hannah," Marc said, turning onto his back and readjusting his newly purchased straw hat so that his eyes were shaded from the brilliant noonday sun.

Hannah nuzzled sleepily against him. "I'm fine." She yawned.

Marc yawned, too. "Can't understand why we're so tired. Can you?"

Hannah laughed, gathering some sand in her hand and letting it trickle down Marc's chest. "No, I can't. But don't count on feeling any more rested tomorrow, babe." She gave a saucy little wink and rolled onto her stomach.

Marc stretched languidly. He thought about his attaché case up in the room and considered going up to the suite to put in a couple of hours of work. Even though he'd told Hannah he wouldn't bring along any work, he'd had to take the Bloomenthal file with him or he'd never have made it down to Philadelphia before that airport, too, got shut down from the snowstorm that was relentlessly traveling south.

He cradled Hannah with one arm and folded his other arm behind his head. Smiling, he remembered Hannah's reaction when she'd spied his attaché case. She'd teased him, playfully scolding him for being a workaholic, and then finally she'd laughed, showing him her briefcase that she'd stowed in one of the bureau drawers.

They were so much alike, he thought. So much in tune with each other. He felt a stirring in his body as he thought about last night, making love with Hannah. Never had he felt so in tune with her as he had then. Hannah had been incredible. He'd never known her to reveal such passionate intensity, such abandon. He had to admit he'd surprised himself as well. Last night, in bed—and out of bed—with Hannah he'd felt remarkably free and daring. Yes, they brought out the best in each other.

He shut his eyes, giving himself up to the drowsiness curling round him, lulled to sleep by the warm sand, the tropical breezes, the jasmine-scented air.

When he awoke, he was stunned to discover he and Hannah had been asleep for close to two hours. Only when he sat up and looked over at Hannah did he realize what a disastrous mistake that had been. He gently nudged Hannah awake.

"I think we'd better get out of the sun, darling. We're both a bit sunburned."

Hannah opened her eyes. A moment later, as she rolled over, she let out a sharp cry. "A bit sunburned? I feel like a lobster." She lifted her sunglasses and examined Marc. "Oh no. You look like a lobster."

Marc tried to smile, but it was more a grimace. "It's nothing. Everybody gets a little burned their first day."

"Right," Hannah said, trying to sound optimistic even as she felt her poor, crisped skin shrinking. "A cold shower, some ointment, we'll be like new in a couple of hours."

THEY WERE ON THEIR SECOND tube of sunburn ointment. Marc gingerly applied another dose to Hannah's bright red back.

"Ow. That hurts," she moaned.

"I'm sorry. Here, is this better?"

"No."

Marc let out a sharp cry as Hannah readjusted her position on the bed, and her foot accidentally brushed against his calf where the skin was already starting to blister. "Really, Hannah, do you have to thrash about?"

"I wasn't thrashing," she snapped. "I couldn't thrash right now even if I wanted to."

"Believe me, I don't want you to."

"You could be a little more sympathetic, Marc."

"I am sympathetic. I am also in pain."

"Well, I'm not feeling exactly perky myself," she retorted tightly. "But I'm still capable of being civil."

"And I'm not?"

"This is dumb. What are we arguing about?" Hannah sighed.

"We weren't arguing."

"Maybe we should go downstairs and eat dinner."

"Only if I can go down there naked," Marc muttered. Neither of them had on a stitch as they lay in bed, Hannah on her stomach, Marc on his back. Their burned skin was so tender that they couldn't bear to put on even the lightest of clothing.

Hannah sighed again. "I guess we should call room service."

"What do you feel like eating?" Marc asked.

"Anything but lobster," Hannah muttered.

A HALF HOUR LATER, when the food arrived, neither of them had any appetite. Hannah picked at her steak; Marc pushed his lamb chops around his plate. Finally Hannah gave up any attempt at eating. She pushed away her plate and gazed wistfully at Marc. "Last night was . . . so perfect."

"There'll be other perfect nights, Hannah."

"I don't think we can even . . . sleep in the same bed tonight. Every time we touch each other we scream in agony." There was a catch in her voice. She was close to tears. And only last night she thought this was the most perfect of honeymoons.

"Don't be sad, Hannah. Look, maybe we should both do a little work for a couple of hours and get our minds off our pain?"

"Work?"

"You did say you had some notes to go over on your Westside park project."

"I do."

"Well, since we can't do much else tonight, we can get our work out of the way, and then tomorrow, when we're feeling better, we'll rent a car and tour the island a little. What do you say, Hannah?"

"I wonder what Dr. Rusman would say?"

"Who's Dr. Rusman?"

Hannah smiled. "It doesn't matter."

Fifteen minutes later, they were each absorbed in their paperwork. When Hannah finished a set of notes, she looked across the bed at Marc and studied him thoughtfully.

He looked up distractedly and gave a quick smile, then focused back on his open file.

"Marc?"

"Mmmm?" He didn't look up.

"Do you think we should have had a more traditional wedding?"

"We had a fine wedding," he muttered as he scribbled a note.

"Don't you feel bad that your family wasn't there?"

"We'll make it up to them."

"How?"

Marc tapped his pen on the file and returned his gaze to Hannah. "Well, I told them we'd get out to see them first chance we got."

"That might not be for weeks, maybe months."

"It's okay. They understand that we're both very busy with our careers."

"Marc?"

"Yes, Hannah?"

"Do you think they'll like me? I mean...do you think they'll think I'm a . . . good enough wife for you?"

Marc set down his pen and smiled at Hannah. "Yes. Better than I deserve."

"Is that what they'd say, or what you say?"

"Both."

"Have you described me to them?"

"Well, yes. I guess I have."

"What did you say? How did you describe me?"

"I said . . . you were very bright." His smile deepened. "You are very bright."

"Right. Bright red."

"Hannah, my parents are going to...adore you. Just like I do."

"You hesitated."

"What?"

"There was a catch in your voice before you said . . . adore."

"Hannah."

"Neither of your sisters has a careers, do they?"

"No, but they both have families."

"They stay home and look after their children, have supper on the table for their hubbies when they get home from a hard day's work."

"You make it sound like it's pure drudgery to be a housewife. My sisters happen to feel very fulfilled. They're active, involved, content."

Hannah's eyes narrowed. "You make it sound like it's pure bliss."

"If that's what you want . . ."

"It's not what *I* want."

"I didn't mean *you* in particular. I was using the general *you*."

"Maybe you meant *you* in particular."

Marc rose from the bed. It was a painful process. "Look, Hannah, I don't expect you to stay home all day cooking my dinner. And as for children, well, we've both agreed to put that off until we're more established. But, I just hope—" He stopped abruptly.

"What do you hope?"

Marc bit off a piece of his cold, tough, leftover lamb chop. He chewed for a moment to give himself time. Hannah tapped her foot impatiently.

"I just hope..." Marc started again, because he knew Hannah wouldn't let him rest until he got it out. Anyway, maybe they should get a few things straight. He decided on a new approach. "We both want to succeed, Hannah."

"Succeed?" She gave him a baffled look, her brow creasing. It hurt too much because of the sunburn, so she unfurrowed it.

"Be successful," he elucidated.

"Well, of course," Hannah said. Being successful was what it was all about.

"I just hope..." He was back where he started. Nothing for it but to spit it out. "I just hope you don't find yourself wanting to compete with me, prove you're as good as me. I mean, you are as good as me, of course. But I just don't want us to get into playing one-upmanship games."

Hannah sprang from the bed, forgetting all about her throbbing skin. "Us? You don't mean us. You mean *me*. You're accusing me—"

"Whoa. I'm not accusing you of anything, Hannah. It's just...sometimes career wives do get...competitive...with their husbands, and I don't want what happened to Ryder and his second wife to happen to us."

Naked, they stood glaring at each other, their faces almost touching. "What about Ryder and his second wife?"

"Let's just say she took the notion of wearing the pants in the family far too literally."

"I think you do wish I was like your sisters, Marc Welles."

"My sisters happen to be very delightful, warm, nurturing women," he retorted.

"I suppose that means I'm grim, cold and selfish?"

"No. You're putting words in my mouth, Hannah."

"You knew when you married me that my career was very important to me, that I had no intention of giving up my work and becoming your hausfrau. I see now that all your talk about supporting my career aspirations was just that—talk. Oh sure, I can have aspirations as long as they don't exceed yours."

"That is not what I'm saying, Hannah," Marc argued, while at the same time wondering how his one simple statement had escalated into a war between them.

"I never thought you were insecure, Marc. I never thought you spent your time worrying about my becoming more successful than you."

"I don't believe this. You haven't understood one word I've said. And I'll tell you why, Hannah Logan." He stopped, pointing a finger at her. "For the same reason you decided not to take my name. For the same reason you refused to move downtown to my apartment. For the same reason you refused to open up a joint bank account. You want to keep the competitive edge. That's why."

"The competitive edge? What does that mean?"

"You know exactly what it means. Your work comes first. You don't want to make any concessions."

"Are you saying that I haven't made a commitment to this marriage?" Hannah's voice threatened to break. She felt awful.

Marc could see her misery in her eyes, in the way her shoulders sagged.

Suddenly contrite, he started to put his arms around her. As soon as his hands lightly touched her shoulders, though, Hannah let out a sharp cry of pain. Marc immediately dropped his hands to his sides.

"Oh, Hannah, we were never going to get into arguments. How did this happen?"

"Maybe we need to spell out the ground rules, have a more . . . formal contract," Hannah suggested.

Marc smiled gently. "We have a pretty formal contract already."

Hannah smiled back, but it was a tentative smile. "It's probably just going to take us some time . . . to adjust."

"Actually," Marc said thoughtfully, "our lives won't really be all that different."

"Unless my mother finds us the perfect midtown apartment in our absence," Hannah pointed out with a modicum of trepidation, which she hoped Marc didn't notice.

He did, but he wasn't about to pick up on it. Not when he was experiencing some trepidation of his own. Instead he said, a smile plastered on his lips, "It'll be wonderful if she does find us a place."

"Yes," Hannah quickly agreed, her manufactured smile matching Marc's perfectly. Yes, a perfect match.

"Of course, it's a tough order finding the right apartment," Marc amended.

"At the right price," Hannah added.

"But then your mother's very persistent."

"Very."

Marc smiled. "Your mother and I had a little heart-to-heart the other night."

"What night?"

"Friday night, after the reception, while you were freshening up."

A wave of anxiety swept over Hannah. "You did? Oh, no. What did she say? No, don't tell me."

"She had some pearls of wisdom to offer me about how to make our marriage a success."

"Why is it," Hannah mused, "so many experts on marriage happen to be divorced?" Hannah sighed. "What did she say?"

Marc grinned. "One of the things she made a big point of was to treat every day together like your honeymoon."

The third day

HANNAH AND MARC DECIDED to hire a guide as well as a car for their last day on St. Croix. The guide, Paul Limetree, turned out to be a gregarious, inquisitive fellow in his early twenties who informed Hannah and Marc that, like them, he, too, was a newlywed.

"So this is your honeymoon, yes?" Paul asked, gazing at them through the rearview mirror as he drove into Christiansted, St. Croix's capital city, an enchanting, beautifully preserved old Danish port.

"Yes," Hannah replied distractedly as she gazed at the pastel-colored, red-roofed eighteenth-century buildings that rimmed the crystal-clear water of the coral-bound bay.

"The wife and I didn't go on a honeymoon. The baby is due any day," Paul informed them. "Anyway, I think the honeymoon maybe isn't such a good thing."

Hannah shot Marc a wry smile. "Well, it has its pluses and negatives, I suppose."

"It's better, I think," offered Paul, "to settle right in, busy yourselves with your home and your chores and your family."

"We don't have a family yet," Marc commented.

"No. We don't plan to have children for a while," Hannah added.

"You don't?" Paul chuckled. "Oh, yes, you should have your babies. It is better when you are young. Lots of babies. The wife and I, we want many babies. How many do you want?"

Hannah looked at Marc. "I don't know. One? Two?"

"One or two?" Paul exclaimed as he swung onto Company Street, an arcaded shopping hub with lacy galleries of iron and wood, decorated with curlicues, cupolas and gingerbread details that reminded Hannah of the Hans Christian Andersen fairy tales. "Oh, no. You should have six or seven. Yes, you have time to have plenty of babies."

"We don't have the time to look after them all. Marc and I both work," Hannah explained. "We're very busy with our careers."

"Oh, my wife, she had a career," Paul said reflectively.

"What did she do?" Marc asked.

"She was a singer. She sang in many of the hotel clubs here. Island music, you know. Very good."

"And now has she given up her career?" Hannah asked.

"Oh, yes. The baby is due any day."

"And after the baby," Hannah persisted.

Paul turned back to Hannah and grinned. "We'll start making another baby."

"Doesn't she mind giving up her singing career to stay home and look after the babies?" Hannah asked, keenly aware of Marc's eyes on her. "After all, if she's talented, she could get some help with the baby and continue developing her career. You could help her. Husbands should take equal responsibility. . . ."

Marc gave Hannah's arm a light squeeze. "It may be different here in St. Croix."

Paul chuckled. "Yes, I think so. Here it's simple. The wife, she looks after the babies and the home, and the husband, he looks after the wife. Now, the wife, she sings to the babies. She's happy, I'm happy. No problems. In the States, I think it's different, yes? Lots of problems. Everybody is getting married, divorced, married, divorced. Nobody is happy. Everybody is mixed-up. The women, they are always so sad. No wonder. They want to be both the woman of the house and the man of the house is what I think."

"Now wait a minute," Hannah said. "There is no reason in the world why a woman can't have a marriage and a career, a family, eventually. It just takes cooperation and a bit of juggling, that's all. Right, Marc?"

Marc gave Hannah a reassuring pat on the arm. "Right. Absolutely right. You just need organization and a clever game plan."

"Exactly," Hannah said. "There are those that say a woman can't have it all, but, personally, I don't see why it should be that difficult."

Paul turned onto Kings' Alley, another street lined with shops. He waved cheerily to some of the locals walking along. "I'll tell you," he said. "There was this nice couple from Chicago I took around the other day. The wife, she tells me she is a schoolteacher and that her husband has brought her here to cheer her up. She says she's been feeling bad since she had her baby."

"Oh, postpartum depression," Hannah elucidated. "That's very common, but it passes. How old is her baby now?"

"Twenty-three years old," Paul answered with a twinkle in his eye. He pulled the car along the curb. "So, you want to go shopping now? I can take you to all the best stores. China, porcelain, coral . . . ? Oh, yes, a souvenir to remember your honeymoon by. This is your first honeymoon, yes?"

5

The Honeymoon's Over

Boardwalk, a restaurant on 74th

HANNAH SHOOK OFF THE SNOW from her black wool coat before hanging it on a hook in the coatroom. She was checking her hair in the mirror when Laura Winninghoff arrived. Coming up behind her, Laura beamed at Hannah's reflection in the mirror.

"There she is, the little bride, still aglow," Laura gushed, leaning closer. "Mmmm. And a new tropical scent. Lovely."

"The *aglow* is sunburn," Hannah muttered dryly. "And the scent isn't eau de cologne. It's eau de sunburn ointment."

"Hmmm. Do I detect a little peevishness?"

Hannah quickly donned a smile. "I must be hungry. I'm always peevish on an empty stomach." She exited the coatroom and headed for the maître d's station, Laura on her heels.

"So, was St. Croix wonderful? Was Marc wonderful? Was—"

"The Quinn party," Hannah said to the maître d', cutting off Laura's inquisition.

"Oh, yes," the tall, thin, elegant man in the black suit said. "The rest of your party is already seated. This way, please."

The maître d' led them through the popular uptown restaurant with its whitewashed walls, umbrellaed tables and beach party decor. The Quinn party had been fortunate to secure a table in the rear where it was a bit more private and where the noise level was reduced to a low hum.

As Hannah and Laura arrived, Diane Quinn and Pam Adams rose from their seats, wineglasses in hand. Laura rushed around Hannah and grabbed another wineglass from the table. All three women extended their glasses in Hannah's direction and began singing off-key, "Here comes the bride . . ."

"Please don't," Hannah pleaded, mortified to hear the maître d' join in for a verse as he handed Hannah her menu.

Pam quieted the group down. "Come on. We're embarrassing Hannah. Anyway, she's not a bride anymore."

"True," Diane seconded. "Now that the honeymoon is over, she's just a plain old wife."

Hannah sat down between Pam and Laura. "Why must you all make such a big deal about my being married? People do it every day."

"We're just jealous," Diane admitted candidly. "I was saying to Pam before you arrived that I think you probably grabbed up the last reasonably terrific bachelor in town. The rest of us are left with the dregs."

"Right," Pam said with a weary little sigh. "The foolish men, the angry men, the fearful men, the men who won't commit...."

"The men who want women who remind them of their mothers," Laura added, eyes raised to the ceiling.

Diane got back into the act. "Meaning men who want you to wait on them hand and foot, boost their egos, tell them how important they are ...?"

"Then there are the ones who have one foot on the bed, one out the door. You know, the slam, bam, thank you, ma'am kind of men." Pam giggled.

"Wait. Wait. Don't forget the newest rage and my personal all-time favorite," Laura announced dramatically. "The men who tell you that they respect your talents and abilities enormously and are quite willing to give you their full moral support as long as you agree in turn to give them your full financial support."

"Was that what made you break it off with that dance instructor?" Diane asked. "He wanted to stay home and look after the plants and let you foot all the bills?"

"He wasn't a dance instructor," Laura said, looking as if she took offense, but then smiling slyly. "He was a dance interpreter. And yes, he was quite eager to be a retired dance interpreter. I gave him the old heave-ho, telling him that me and my plants would somehow manage to survive on our own, thank you."

"See how lucky you are, Hannah?" Pam said enviously, but as she saw the wilted smile on Hannah's face, she grew immediately concerned. As did the others.

"What's the matter, Hannah?" Pam asked softly.

"No-nothing. Nothing's the matter."

Diane's eyes narrowed. "The post-honeymoon blues?"

Post nothing, Hannah thought. "I guess," she said aloud.

"And poor Hannah got sunburned down in St. Croix," Laura offered. In the dimly lit dining area, Hannah's sunburn didn't show.

"Oh, no," Pam said sympathetically. "Did Marc get burned, too?"

Hannah nodded glumly.

"Why, the same thing happened to me and Don on our honeymoon in Jamaica," Laura commented. "It was ghastly. We got burned to a crisp and had to put passion on hold for two nights."

"We only had three nights," Hannah pointed out. "Let's just say that one of them was definitely a cut above the others." She felt her cheeks heat up just remembering.

"Next honeymoon, I'm going someplace cold," Laura decided.

"Like Alaska?" quipped Diane.

Pam grinned. "Snuggled into a sleeping bag in some little igloo, rubbing noses and . . . whatever. I don't know. It sounds pretty cosy."

"Actually I was thinking more of some place like Paris or Venice," Laura said dreamily. "I'd much prefer to do my snuggling in a gondola than an igloo." Laura leaned forward in her seat and cast the group a conspiratorial smile. "Did I tell you, I met this absolutely gorgeous male model at a cocktail party Saturday night?"

"Oh, please," Pam said acerbically, "spare us. Male models are so vain and egotistical, Laura. Any expert worth his salt would tell you that models are definite no-no's for any kind of meaningful relationships."

"And given the fact that you have a healthy ego yourself, Laura," Diane pointed out good-humoredly, "it could get ugly."

"You're such a pessimist, Diane," Laura countered, although she was smiling. "Is there a law that says a man can't be caring and sensitive, even if he is gorgeous. Look at Marc. He's certainly damn eye-catching and yet he's incredibly caring and sensitive, isn't he, Hannah? And he thinks you're God's gift to women, I bet," Laura said, sighing.

All eyes turned to the newlywed. Hannah looked uneasily around the table. "Yes, yes, of course Marc's caring and sensitive. It's just . . . it's just . . . he has this crazy notion that . . . I'm too . . . too competitive. I mean, he doesn't think I am yet. But that I might get to be. Like Ryder's second wife." Having said more than she'd meant to, Hannah abruptly opened her menu and pulled it up to her face. "So, what's good to eat?"

"Who's Ryder?" Laura asked, puzzled.

Diane raised a brow. "Who's his second wife?"

"Ryder's Marc's boss," Pam elucidated, taking Hannah's hand. "A three-time loser. I don't know about the second wife, but I once met his third wife. His third ex-wife, I should say. She didn't seem too broken up about the divorce. She had a few choice words for the much-married Ryder, but I can't say them in public."

Laura's expression remained puzzled. "So, what's Marc's problem, Hannah?" she asked. "Is he afraid you'll outrank or outearn him or something?"

Diane scowled. "Oh, yes, the men who can't cope with a woman's success. We forgot about that group, ladies. I hope you're not going to knuckle under, Hannah."

"On the other hand," Laura piped in, "I don't think it's ever wise to make a man feel...inadequate. Men are such vulnerable creatures at heart."

Diane snickered. "They're vulnerable? Oh, please, Laura. Men have a thing about having to be in control, maintaining the upper hand—"

"That's because men are basically insecure," Pam broke in.

"Let's face it," Diane declared. "Peel away the veneer and men are still your standard make male chauvinist pigs."

"Diane, the phrase *male chauvinist pig* went out with the eighties. Besides, men are not pigs," Pam said earnestly. "It's just harder for them to reveal their true selves because men's liberation from male-dominated roles has not kept up with women's lib. Did you ever read the Kenwood book, *If I'm Not a Man, What Am I?* Kenwood gives this brilliant analysis of why—"

Hannah, growing more tense by the moment, slammed her menu shut, sending a breeze around the table. "I'm having the pig roast...I mean pot roast." She paused. "Well done."

An apartment for rent in midtown Manhattan

MARC RUSHED DOWN the street to where Hannah was impatiently waiting outside the art deco facade of a twelve-story apartment building. She checked her watch just as he arrived.

"I know, I know," he said in a breathless apologetic tone. "Try getting a cab at four o'clock. . . ."

"Four-fifteen was the only appointment time my mother could get. There are already three other couples interested in renting. Mother managed to turn on the charm and get the superintendent to give us a look." She turned away from Marc to buzz the superintendent's apartment, but before her finger hit the button, Marc grabbed her.

"Hey."

Hannah turned around and found herself wrapped in Marc's arms. "Hey," she whispered back.

Marc kissed her lightly on the lips. "Are we going to have dinner together tonight?"

Hannah sighed. "Oh, Marc, I can't. I've got the mayor's dinner tonight, remember? But I tell you what. Since I'll be downtown anyway, I'll spend tonight at your place."

"That's probably not such a good idea. By the time you sit through all the after-dinner speeches, you won't get out of there until close to midnight, and I've got to be up by six in the morning to make it out to Long Island."

Hannah nodded. "Oh, right, you told me about that meeting. Well . . . we'll have dinner tomorrow night."

"I won't be back from the Island until nine, maybe ten tomorrow night."

Hannah attempted a bright smile as she pressed the entry buzzer. "Let's hope this place is as great as Mother says it is. At least then we'll get to be strangers passing in the night."

"Even if the place isn't great," Marc said, opening the glass and iron door as the buzzer went off, "let's take it if it's at least workable."

TEN MINUTES LATER Hannah and Marc stared glumly at each other in the middle of the empty living room.

"What was my mother thinking?" Hannah muttered.

"Didn't you tell her we need at least two bedrooms, ideally three? There's no room for even one of us to set up an at-home office here," Marc pointed out.

"I know. And only one bath."

"There was one? I thought that was the slop closet," Marc said facetiously.

"The kitchen's not bad. If you want to overlook the cockroaches that were already cooking dinner in there."

Marc grinned. "Whatever they were making, it didn't smell too good."

"Oh, Marc." Hannah fell limply against his chest, draping her arms around his neck. "I can't live here. I just can't."

"We'll keep looking, Hannah. We'll find something eventually. And we both agreed, didn't we, that we would deal with these matters very practically and pragmatically?"

Hannah nodded. "Right. No added pressure, no desperate measures. We'll be sensible, reasonable."

"Give me a big kiss, Hannah."

"It can't be too big. My lips are still burned."

He gently smoothed back her hair. "It wasn't much of a honeymoon, was it?"

Hannah kissed Marc lightly. "The first night in St. Croix was pretty terrific."

Marc smiled crookedly. "Even if you did mistake me for Bloomenthal."

"I gave Bloomenthal what he deserved," Hannah quipped, edging her hand inside Marc's jacket. "And then I gave you, Marc Welles, what you deserved." Her hand inched down to the waistband of his trousers.

"Don't you have to get home to change for the mayor's dinner?" Halfway through the sentence, the breath caught in Marc's throat as Hannah's fingers moved lower.

"I'm a fast changer. And the superintendent did tell us when he gave us the key we could take as much time up here as we needed. Oh, Marc," Hannah whispered, wriggling out of her coat, "I...need...time." She closed her eyes and let the sensation of desire sweep over her as she attacked Marc's belt buckle.

"Shall we christen all the apartments we look at this way?" Marc murmured, working eagerly on the buttons of Hannah's blouse.

"Mmmm. Yes, every one of them." She unzipped his trousers, tugging them down his legs as Marc worked on her skirt. They both dropped to their knees on the parquet floor, helping each other get rid of their extraneous garments.

Marc hurriedly made a blanket of Hannah's coat and pulled her with him on top of it. "Oh, Hannah, let's look at apartments every day."

He kissed her mouth, her neck, her shoulders, his hands gently cupping her breasts. "I love your lovely, soft, perky breasts, Hannah. I'm so glad you didn't go topless down in St. Croix and get them all sunburned. They're so dear. So beautiful. So tasty," he whispered as his tongue circled first one nipple then the other.

Hannah shivered with wanton delight. She sought his lips, kissing him greedily, forgetting all about her sunburn and his. "Marc, I want you. I want you so much."

"And I want you. . . ." His hands explored the curves of her body, his mouth returning to do wondrous things to her nipples.

Hannah was wild by this time, caressing her husband's body with open abandon. It felt wonderfully illicit, making love on impulse in the barren apartment. Wave after wave of heat rose in her belly; she wanted more, more, more. Thrusting her hips upward, she strained against him as he glided his hand down over her buttocks, slipping inside her.

She drew one leg over his hip, her heart slamming against the walls of her chest as their intimate rhythm picked up pace and intensity.

Marc sought her lips, his mouth opening over hers, his hands coming up to each side of her face. With each thrust he murmured her name. "Hannah, Hannah." Uninhibited moans of pleasure escaped Hannah's lips. She flung her head back, eyes closed, as she was engulfed in sensations, every fiber of her body exuding a sexual energy and heat. She was on the edge of control, and then, completely submerged in the rhythm of their bodies, she lost it. They both cried out, Marc's own pleasure reaching its fevered pitch along with her.

They were so involved in the expression of their mutual release they almost didn't hear the front doorbell.

Hannah gasped as she heard the superintendent call out their names.

"How are you two coming along?" came the husky voice through the door.

Racing about the living room, throwing on their clothes, they both called back, "Oh, fine. Fine. Almost done."

"If you got any questions . . ."

"No, no," Marc shouted, pulling on his trousers only to see Hannah holding up his boxer shorts.

The superintendent chose that moment to unlock the door and step in. Hannah hastily stuffed Marc's boxers inside her blouse. Amazingly enough, as the superintendent entered the living room Hannah and Marc looked almost presentable. Hannah was shrugging on her coat, fanning herself with her hand.

"Hot in here, isn't it?" she muttered.

The superintendent shrugged. "Most of the tenants have no complaint about the heat."

"Oh, she's not complaining," Marc said quickly, feeling awkward without any underwear.

"Oh, no, I'm not complaining," Hannah concurred.

"So, what you think of the apartment?" the superintendent inquired.

"Well," Hannah said, trying to surreptitiously straighten the seams of her skirt, "it's a bit . . . small. Right, darling?"

Marc nodded, taking Hannah's hand. "Yes. Nice but . . . small."

"You got a good-sized living room here," the superintendent pointed out.

"Oh, the living room is . . . the best feature of the apartment," Hannah agreed enthusiastically. "We love the living room. This is just a perfect living room."

"Yes, I don't think we've ever felt more . . . content . . . in any other living room," Marc said with a smile. "It's just that we're . . . undecided. We need to . . . discuss it."

"Maybe we could come back and . . . take a second look?" Hannah asked, giving Marc a saucy smile.

The superintendent rubbed his jaw. "Well, I told your mother I got three other interested parties. Most likely one of them's gonna take it before the week's out."

Mark put his arm around Hannah and guided her to the door. "We can't tell you how much we appreciate your letting us . . . uh . . . look around. We enjoyed ourselves thoroughly." He opened the door.

"Yes," Hannah said, stepping into the hall. "We loved every minute of it."

The superintendent shrugged as he watched them head, hand in hand, toward the elevator. "I'll tell you, if you have such a great time looking at a place you don't wanna rent, I bet you two'll be just tickled pink when you find the one you do want."

Hannah and Marc were both laughing hard as they stepped into the elevator. Who would have ever thought apartment hunting could be such fun?

CSR offices

MARC WAS REVIEWING the Vysco account spreadsheet when Harris Porter came up behind him.

"Hey, I hear you backed out of the Morrisey dinner on Wednesday, Marc."

"Oh . . . yeah. I can't make it," Marc muttered, checking some figures that didn't mesh.

"I hope you've got a good excuse. You know how Ryder feels about Morrisey. He likes to show the old man what a slick-looking, tidy little ship he runs. And we're Ryder's trusty shipmates."

"I know, but I promised Hannah over two weeks ago that I'd set aside this Wednesday night. Her mother's throwing a dinner party for us. And she's also dying for us to meet some new guy she's met."

Harris Porter smiled slyly as he came around and perched himself on the corner of Marc's desk. "So, the old ball and chain's got you jumping hoops already. You sure it's dinner and not obedience training?"

Marc looked up from his work and glared at Harris. "Come off it. Hannah and I haven't had a night out together since we got back from St. Croix. It never fails. If both of us aren't busy, at least one of us is. Even the weekends have gotten fouled up. Last weekend, Hannah had to go to Washington for a conference and the weekend before I had to wine and dine Bloomenthal."

"Yeah, it's tough, but if I were you, pal, I wouldn't be the one making the first concessions. Once you do, then you'll be expected to be the one to always make them. I've seen Hannah in operation, Marc. She's a real hotshot when it comes to her career. Do you really think she'd give up an important meeting to go to your mother's house for dinner?"

"My mother lives in Minnesota," Marc muttered. "And you're wrong about Hannah not making concessions."

"Oh, yeah? Name three."

"Okay," Marc said. "Three." He paused. "Let's see. There was . . . well, that wasn't really a concession. . . ."

"Name one," Harris suggested with a wiseacre grin.

Marc frowned. *A concession* . . .

Harris laughed. "Forget it, Marc."

"No," Marc snapped. "I don't want you thinking Hannah doesn't make concessions. It's just that it hasn't come up—"

"Until now," Harris pointed out. "Until she ordered you to show up at her momma's on Wednesday night."

"Come off it, Harris. That's not the way it was. Hannah didn't issue any orders. And if I wanted to cancel out, she'd be perfectly understanding."

Harris leaned a little closer. "Give it up, Marc. It's every married guy's fate. You know, there's this old joke. When married men die, and they go up to heaven, they discover that instead of arriving at the Pearly Gates, there are these two doors. One of them's labeled Manly Men and the other's labeled Mousey Men. So, one time, St. Peter comes out and he's not surprised to see the long row of married men lined up in front of the Mousey Men door. But then he sees this one solitary married guy standing in front of the door marked Manly Men. St. Peter's real impressed, so he goes over to this guy and asks him how come he had the mettle to stand in front of the door marked Manly Men. The married guy shrugs his shoulders and he says to St. Peter, 'I don't know. My wife told me to stand here.'"

452 Grammercy Park

"HANNAH, YOU'RE EARLY. You look dreadful. Where's Marc?"

"And good evening to you, too, Mother," Hannah replied acerbically. "Am I the first one to arrive?"

"Why, yes. The invitation was for seven-thirty and it's just a little past six. You're never early for my get-togethers. You're never even on time for my get-togethers. What's wrong? Did you and Marc have a fight?"

"No . . ."

"Right. I forgot. You never fight. You're both too rational and reasonable to fight. However, if you want my opinion—"

"Not really."

"I think you two don't fight because you never see each other. He isn't coming tonight, is he?"

"No," Hannah said succinctly, hanging her coat in the closet.

"Did the two of you look at that apartment I saw listed in the papers over on 54th Street?"

"I ran over to see it. Marc couldn't get away." Hannah tried to conceal the disappointment in her voice. "We've both been too busy to look at any apartments together."

"Well, what did you think of the place on 54th?" Mary Logan asked, following her daughter into the living room.

"It was better than some."

"Well . . . ?"

"It was on the second floor. Marc prefers to be on an upper floor. He thinks there's less risk of a break-in."

"It's a high-security building, Hannah."

"It was kind of dark. Faced onto a taller building that blocked out the sun."

Mary Logan watched as her daughter poured herself a glass of wine and nibbled on an endive leaf stuffed with a garlicy cheese spread. "Do you want to know what I think, Hannah?"

Hannah sighed. "Why do you always ask me if I want to know what you think when you don't pay any attention when I say I don't want to know?"

"Because I know, my dear, that deep down, you do," Mary said softly, taking a seat on the sofa beside her daughter and gently rubbing off a spot of cheese spread from the corner of Hannah's lip. "Isn't that why you showed up early tonight?"

"No." Hannah finished up the endive leaf and reached for another.

"Hannah, you have always hated endive."

Hannah stared down at the green leafy vegetable. "I still do."

Mary took a long, close look at her daughter. "Admitting you're feeling terrified, darling, might be a good start."

"Terrified of what? A good start at what?"

"Terrified of being married. A good start at being married."

"You don't understand. It was different in your day."

"Women worked in my day. I worked the first three years your father and I were married." She emitted a little laugh. "Of course, he didn't."

"It's just a busy time for both of us right now. It isn't that we don't want to spend more time together. Take tonight." Hannah stopped, suddenly overwhelmed by a desire to cry.

Mary Logan took the endive out of Hannah's hand, then took her daughter's hand in hers. "Even when a husband and wife have busy schedules, Hannah, they have to make time for each other."

"I do make time," Hannah snapped. "Tonight was going to be our time together. We both agreed. We were both looking forward to coming here. And then, after it's all set, two days ago Marc tells me he's got to cancel out. He tells me he has some important function his boss expects him to attend."

"Well, that happens to both of you at times," Mary soothed.

"It wasn't his canceling out that got me so upset. It was the way he did it. He was so abrupt, so . . . rude about it. And then, out of nowhere, he tells me this absolutely obnoxious joke about married men that he'd heard at the office. After which he looks at me very meaningfully and says, 'Get the point.'" Hannah sighed. "If the point was that Marc's a lousy, insulting comic, I got it."

"Hannah, your father used to tell rotten jokes, too."

"And what did you do, Mother? Laugh anyway?"

"No. Actually I divorced him." Mary Logan saw the grim look on her daughter's face, and smiled. "Darling, I was joking. Maybe, you should learn to laugh a little. A sense of humor can go a long way in a marriage."

6

The Fine Art of Juggling

Hannah's uptown apartment

THE PHONE WAS RINGING as Hannah stepped into her apartment. She dumped her bag on the hall table and got the phone in her bedroom on the fourth ring.

"Hi," a familiar voice greeted her.

"Marc?" She shrugged out of her coat and kicked her shoes off.

"You sound surprised."

Hannah cleared her throat and checked her watch. It was a few minutes past ten. "I thought you'd be tied up until...later." She could hear the awkward, tight sound of her voice. This was so dumb. Whatever happened to those best laid plans?

"I just got back home. What about you?" Marc asked.

"Me too."

"Hannah..."

"Marc..." Hannah said at the same time.

They both laughed.

"You go first," Marc said softly.

"Oh...it's just...I suppose..." Hannah stopped. "You probably won't remember this, but in my prenuptial days I was really quite articulate."

Marc laughed. "I remember, darling. It wasn't all that long ago."

"Oh, Marc, nothing seems to be going the way I thought it would. I shouldn't have given you such a hard time about the Morrisey meeting. Let's face it, if the shoe were on the other foot, I would have begged off a family dinner for business." What she didn't add was that it would have made her miserable and more than likely she'd have come back home and had herself a good cry after the meeting.

Marc, who had been all ready with an apology for canceling out on dinner at his mother-in-law's, stopped short. "You would have?"

"What I'm saying is, this work-marriage business isn't easy. I guess I didn't realize how much of a juggling act it was going to be."

"I know," Marc admitted. "I thought that since we've both been so successful at our careers, we were bound to be successful at marriage."

"We just have to work a little harder," Hannah said, fighting back tears.

"Right," Marc said glumly. "A little more careful organization and structure . . ."

"There's no reason we can't have the best of both worlds." Hannah tried to inject a note of confidence in her voice.

There was an awkward silence. And they both rushed in at the same time to fill it.

"So how was the meeting . . . ?"

"So how was your mother's dinner party . . . ?"

"The meeting," Marc answered first, "was a bore, but Ryder was in his glory with all of his boys in attendance." There was a brief pause. "And his new gal."

Hannah duly noted the pause. She also immediately adjusted her voice to that of cool reflection. "Oh, you mean Robin Corbett was there? I thought she was still on vacation and wouldn't be starting at CSR until next week."

"Officially. But, this was sort of her warm-up."

"I bet she warmed things up, all right," Hannah said wryly, remembering her one and only encounter with the smart, tough and incredibly attractive Robin Corbett a couple of months ago at a dinner party celebrating her appointment at CSR. Robin, from L.A., had that certain California panache and insouciant glamour that enabled her to really work a crowd. Hannah had been both impressed and envious. Not to mention that Robin Corbett's appointment at CSR had been quite a coup. Robin would be the only female senior accounts' executive on staff. Marc, Harris Porter and John Moss, along with their boss, Doug Ryder, seemed tickled pink to have Robin on board.

"Robin was great tonight," Marc said, not masking his admiration. "She wrapped old Morrisey around her little finger."

Hannah idly held out her free hand and examined her fingers. "So now Robin's got all five fingers accounted for," she muttered, thinking of Marc, his boss, and his other two colleagues, all four of whom Robin had already worked her magic on.

"What?" Marc said, not getting the point of Hannah's remark.

"Nothing."

"Robin remembered you, by the way. And sent you
her best." Marc emitted a little laugh. "She asked me if
we were living together now. I said, 'No, we're married.' Harris and John thought it was very funny, but
Robin didn't get the joke until Harris explained that we
still haven't found an apartment yet. Robin was wholly
sympathetic. She's having her own struggles finding a
decent place to live in town. Right now, she's holed up
with an old college friend of hers over on East 38th
Street. I told her that if we find an apartment soon, she
could sublet mine. She's . . . uh . . . going to come over
tomorrow after work to . . . check it out."

Hannah felt a distinct twinge of discomfort. "Tomorrow night?"

"Yes. Oh, Robin was hoping you could join us. She'd
love to see you again. She really liked you, Hannah."

"I'll be tied up in meetings till past seven tomorrow
night, but how thoughtful of Robin to think of me,"
Hannah said archly.

"Well, I thought of you, too, darling," Marc rushed
on to say. And then after a pause he added, "I think of
you night and day, Hannah. It's showing in my work.
I don't seem able to concentrate like I used to. I keep remembering that incredible afternoon we spent in that
empty apartment."

Hannah closed her eyes. She, too, had spent many a
day and night remembering that brief but oh so intox-
icating interlude. "We haven't both looked at another
apartment together since then," Hannah said wistfully, curling her legs up on the bed and switching the
receiver to her other side. "I love you so much, Marc."

"I love you, too."

They were both silent for a moment. Then Marc asked, "How was your night, Hannah?"

"I spent most of the evening chatting with Mother's new beau, Simon Potter."

"What was he like?" Marc asked, loosening his tie as he stretched out on the bed and propped another pillow behind his head.

"Oh, he was charming, urbane, quite attractive. He used to own a group of travel agencies, but he's retired now. He's very much a world traveler. He's also been married four times."

"Four times? Not a great track record. What's your mother's feeling about that?"

Hannah laughed. "She's utterly calm and relaxed about it. In fact, she joked with me privately that if she were to marry again, she'd just as soon hitch up with someone who'd been married before since she'd be doing her bit for recycling."

Marc chuckled. "I like your mother."

"Yeah, I like her, too," Hannah said with a smile. "So does Simon." She propped another pillow behind her head. "Maybe they will get married."

"How will you feel about it, if they do?"

"I don't know," Hannah said honestly. "Maybe, between them, after so much trial and error, they'd get it right this time."

"Where does that leave us?" Marc asked in a low, disquieted voice.

Hannah sighed. "We're going to be the exception to the rule, Marc. We're going to get it right the first time."

Or die trying, she thought as she hung up the receiver after sending Marc a good-night kiss.

Hannah sat up, swung her legs over the side of the bed and stared at the phone. Desire and frustration crackled along her skin. What was she doing sending kisses to her husband over the telephone when she wanted to be planting warm, moist, eager kisses all over his body? This was no way to get their marriage right. Being married wasn't just organization and scheduling; it wasn't just being understanding and giving each other wide berths; it wasn't discipline and logic, at least not the kind of logic that seemed to work so well for Hannah in her career. Marriage, Hannah was slowly coming to learn, had a unique logic all its own. Or maybe it wasn't logical at all. Maybe it was the very absence of logic that left Hannah feeling at such a loss.

A deep line furrowed her brow. Logic told her that when in doubt, think it out. But along with the voice of reason came another equally persistent voice that argued for a different strategy. When in doubt, take a chance. Be impulsive. Reach out and touch . . . and, contrary to the popular ads, not over the telephone.

Without giving herself time to think it through, Hannah wriggled her feet back into her shoes and threw her coat on. So what if it was late for a weekday night. So what if she had to be up at the crack of dawn. So what if getting a cab to work tomorrow was going to be a hassle. . . .

Hannah grabbed her pocketbook and flew out the front door. *Oh, Marc, darling, love, I'm coming. I'll be with you very soon, my dearest. . . .*

Twenty minutes later, breathless and awash with excitement, Hannah used her key to get into Marc's apartment. Once inside, so as not to alarm him, she called out. "It's me, Marc. Hannah. I've come to give you that kiss good-night in person, darling." As she spoke, she crossed the living room and flung open the door to Marc's bedroom. "Surprise, darling. Move over and make room for me. I'm spending the night with you. Wake up, sleepyhead, or shall I—" She stopped abruptly as she got to the bed. "Marc?"

She switched on the lamp. Hannah stared at the empty bed, puzzled. Where was Marc? He'd been here twenty minutes ago. She sat on the edge of the bed. Maybe, she thought, he'd run down the street to the all-night grocery store to pick up a few items he might need for the next day. Hannah frowned. Maybe he was getting some wine and cheese for his after-work get-together tomorrow with the dazzling Ms. Robin Corbett.

Hannah sighed, feeling a flash of shame. It wasn't like her to be jealous and distrustful. And Marc had certainly never given her cause to be concerned about his fidelity. It did make perfect sense, she had to admit, for Robin to be interested in Marc's apartment, and Hannah knew it wasn't fair to presume that Robin had an equal interest in her husband. Still, Hannah wondered what Robin made of the fact that she and Marc weren't living together. Maybe Robin saw their living situation as a sign that the marriage was more of a business arrangement than one of passion. If Robin did think that, and if she was, after all, interested in Marc, she might feel it was okay to go after him.

Hannah's mind started racing. Would Marc ever succumb to the no doubt brilliant, seductive maneuvers of the wanton, willful, manipulative Robin Corbett? Would frustration and doubt drive him into Robin's outstretched arms? Was he wrapped in those arms at this very minute? Having tossed off an over-the-phone-line good-night kiss to his wife, had her deceitful, unfaithful husband rushed off into the night for an assignation with *the other woman?* Oh, no, Hannah thought with despair, married not even two months and cuckolded already. No, that wasn't right. Only husbands could be cuckolded. Okay, so what were wives? Trusting idiots, that's what, Hannah decided.

And then she stopped herself short. What was she doing playing out this wholly irrational melodrama? Any minute now, Marc would come strolling back into his apartment with a bag full of groceries, and here she was imagining her dear innocent husband off having illicit meaningless sex with some office bimbo!

Hannah laughed aloud, threw off her coat, kicked off her shoes and started stripping out of the rest of her clothes. Wouldn't Marc be surprised when he walked into his bedroom and found his wife lying in bed in all her naked glory just waiting to recreate the best moments of their earlier interlude in that empty apartment? Hannah rushed into the bathroom to take a fast shower. She wanted to be fresh as a daisy when Marc crawled into bed beside her. Feeling a flush of exaltation and arousal, Hannah pinned up her hair and stepped under the pulsating spray.

MARC LET THE PHONE at his apartment ring a half-dozen times before hanging up. So much for logic. He sat down on Hannah's bed, wondering where his wife could have run off to at this hour of the night if not to his apartment. He'd been so sure she'd gone there. While he'd dialed his own number, he'd even chuckled at the irony of Hannah taking off for his apartment while he'd grabbed a cab and come to hers. But if she hadn't gone there, where had she gone?

He felt a flash of alarm as he gave Hannah's bedroom a careful scrutiny. Could someone have broken into the apartment and absconded with his wife? But there was no sign of a struggle and Hannah was not the sort of woman to give in without one. No, there had to be a less distressing solution.

Or, Marc thought uneasily, one that was distressing for altogether different reasons. Could Hannah secretly be involved with a lover? Had their marriage already failed so miserably that his wife of less than two months was already seeking solace and sex in the arms of another man?

Marc started pacing the bedroom, replaying his last phone conversation with Hannah. She'd sounded strange on the phone, unable to express herself cogently at times, snippy, a bit distant. And then there'd been the clear note of sarcasm in Hannah's voice when he'd mentioned Robin Corbett.

Sweat broke out across Marc's brow. Did Hannah think that he, too, would fool around on the sly? Marc's jaw muscles tightened. How could Hannah cheat on him? How could she tell him not a half hour ago that they were going to make their marriage work, and then no sooner had she hung up the phone, taken off to spend the rest of the night with her lover?

Marc could feel his whole body tremble in outrage and despair. He was working himself up into quite a frenzy. And then, suddenly, a flash of reason intervened. There could be a far more innocent reason for Hannah's disappearance. Yes, she'd been upset and not quite herself on the phone. And who did Hannah turn to when she was upset? Her best friend, Pam Adams, who lived only a few streets away. Yes, of course, Marc thought, relief washing over him. He checked his watch. It wasn't all that late, after all. Hannah could have zipped over to Pam's for a little female heart-to-heart. It made all the sense in the world. Give or take an hour, his loving, innocent wife would be returning to her apartment, hopefully feeling a bit better.

Marc smiled. He knew how to make Hannah feel much better. Much, much better. Stripping off his clothes, Marc headed for the shower. When Hannah did return home, she'd find her loving husband under the covers waiting for her with open arms.

HANNAH LET THE PHONE RING at her apartment four times, clicking off when her answer machine came on. Damn, she thought, slamming the receiver into the cradle. So much for logical thinking. . . .

Marc's downtown apartment

ROBIN CORBETT did a slow pirouette around the living room. "Marc, it's terrific. Not just the apartment itself, but the way you've fixed it up. I'm crazy about the

Berber carpeting, and I love the way you combined neo-modern with Tudor. But you must have had a decorator help you. With your schedule, surely you didn't put this all together yourself?"

Marc quirked a smile at his ebullient new colleague. "It's nothing, really. I just went over to one of the department stores, walked through the furniture section, pointed out what I wanted and had it all delivered."

"You're too modest, Marc."

"You really like it?"

"Yes. Oh, yes. I adore the apartment, the decor. I know this is digging my own grave, but I don't understand how you could give this pearl up. I mean, you can even walk to CSR. No hassles with cabs . . ."

"Tell me about it," Marc muttered. He'd spent the entire night at Hannah's apartment waiting for her to show up. He couldn't believe she'd not only spent the entire night someplace else, but hadn't even come home to change her clothes in the morning. Or, at least, she hadn't shown up by seven when he'd had to finally leave to catch a cab back to his apartment to change his clothes and get to work.

While Marc was ruminating, Robin Corbett was studying him with interest. "Is this a bad time, Marc?"

Bad wasn't the word for it. "Sorry," he said quietly. "I didn't sleep well last night."

"When I have a lousy night, I'm always a wreck the next day. It's hard to concentrate," Robin said sympathetically.

Marc sat down on his off-white Tudor-style sofa. "I guess it was pretty obvious I wasn't exactly at my winning best at work today."

Robin walked over to Marc and placed a hand lightly on his shoulder. "We all have days like that. And I guess, in your situation—"

Marc looked up sharply. "What do you mean, my situation?"

Robin held up her hand in apology. "Sorry. I just meant, being married, it must be that much more difficult to find the time and energy for both your personal and professional life. It must be quite a challenge learning how to juggle them both without dropping one of the balls."

A deep sigh escaped Marc's lips as he leaned back and let his head drop on the cushion. "Juggling, huh?"

Marc's eyes were closed and he started when he felt Robin's cool hand on his brow.

"You're so tense, Marc. Is it that rough?" Robin asked softly.

Marc was sorely tempted to tell Robin just how rough it was. If he wasn't so afraid to admit it, he was tempted to do more than spill forth his marital problems to this soothing, understanding, gentle and very attractive colleague of his. But he pulled himself together, knowing that he wasn't going to say or do anything at all. Whatever problems he and Hannah were having, Marc knew that it was only going to be resolved between Hannah and himself.

At least a dozen times today at work, he'd picked up the phone to call Hannah at her office and have it out with her. Surely she had some simple explanation about where she'd spent the night. And wouldn't he feel mighty silly when she told him she'd fallen asleep over at Pam's. Or maybe even at her mother's apartment.

So, if he was so sure of Hannah's innocence, why hadn't he phoned her instead of tormenting himself all day with so many guilty possibilities? Yes, why indeed?

"Do you want to show me around the rest of the apartment, Marc, or would you rather I come back another time?"

Marc had almost forgotten about Robin. Robin with the soft voice, the cool hands, the tantalizing scent. He fantasized that her perfume had a name like Temptation or Fascination, or something simpler, more basic, like, Take Me, I'm Yours for the Asking. He sprang from the sofa. "Sorry. Of course, I'll finish showing you the apartment, Robin. How about the kitchen?"

Robin followed his lead. "Now, Marc, how many bedrooms did you say you have here?"

"Just the one," he mumbled. "But there's a den that you could convert to a spare bedroom."

They were walking down the hall to the kitchen when they neared a closed door off to the right.

"Is that the den in there?" Robin asked.

"Uh . . . no. That's my bedroom."

Robin came to a halt at the door. "Well, why don't we check the bedroom out next . . . since we're right here?"

A jet of panic washed over Marc. This is crazy, he told himself as he stood frozen in the hallway as Robin walked into his bedroom. The woman, he told himself firmly, couldn't be making a pass at him. She was simply interested in checking out the whole apartment. Any prospective renter would want to see the bedroom.

"Marc, this is terrific. What a bright, spacious room," Robin called out enthusiastically.

Marc hesitated and then walked in. "It's kind of...messy," he muttered. "I was...uh...out late last night."

"You have impeccable taste, Marc. Are you thinking of selling any of the furniture? This bed is great. I love the woven wood effect on the headboard. And I definitely want a queen-size bed. This is queen-size, isn't it?" As she asked the question, she plunked down on the bed, testing out the mattress. "Firm. I'm just like you. I must have a firm mattress."

To Marc's chagrin, Robin Corbett stretched out lengthwise on the bed, with only her feet, which were ensconced in expensive leather pumps, hanging off the edge. "I can't imagine how you don't sleep well every night on a bed like this," she murmured. "If you could see what I've been sleeping on for the last week. One of those dreadful fold-out couches. What I wouldn't give—" She stopped abruptly and giggled. "Sorry. I am going on, aren't I?"

She propped herself up on her elbows and smiled at Marc. "Are you uncomfortable?"

"Me? No. No."

"Hannah's a very lucky woman. I hope she knows that."

"Robin . . ."

"If you were free, Marc, I'd grab you up in a minute." She blushed on cue. "God, that sounds terribly presumptuous of me, thinking you'd want me grabbing you up. Would you?"

Marc's blush was purely involuntary. "What?"

Robin laughed. "I like you this way. Kind of awkward, unsure of yourself, nervous. Don't get me wrong. I like that strong, self-confident, take-charge part of you, too. I wouldn't be surprised if you're the next VP at CSR. You've got smarts, drive, ambition, and you're incredibly attractive. Don't think looks don't count. They count in this game for both men *and* women. Unfortunately, looks count against a woman more often than not, whereas it's just the opposite for a man. Beautiful women can be distracting. Good-looking men inspire confidence. Just being around you, Marc, inspires me."

"Well . . . thanks. Thank you, Robin. But . . ."

"Marc, I know it's none of my business, but can I give you a piece of free advice?"

"Well . . . sure. You might as well. It seems, lately, I inspire more advice than confidence."

"Sometimes, when the juggling gets too tough, it can help to take a break. Just get away from the pressures for a while. Let yourself be distracted. Do you follow?" Robin leaned her head against the headboard, her blue-eyed gaze fixed on Marc.

"I'm . . . uh . . . not sure," Marc muttered, feeling incredibly uncomfortable, and yet fascinated at the same.

Robin wet her lips. "Let's face it, Marc. It's a shrinking market out there. Like the saying goes, the good men always get grabbed up fast." She paused, smiled, wet her lips again, and went on. "I'm going to lay my cards on the table. I've had some very successful . . . relationships . . . with married men. Believe me, there are several wives in L.A. who have me to thank for the survival of their marriages. A flagging mar-

riage can definitely profit, operationally, from a good
affair. You're too shrewd a businessman not to come to
that conclusion sooner or later, Marc. I'd like it to be
sooner. And I'd like to be the one you go with. It would
be fun, convenient, and I wouldn't be surprised if we
both don't prosper professionally as well as personally
from the experience." Having concluded her sales pitch,
Robin leaned back on Marc's pillow and waited for him
to make the next move.

Marc smiled. "You're certainly direct, Robin. And if
I was up for grabs . . . But, I'm not. Whatever problems
Hannah and I may be having, I love her. And I guess
I'm naive enough to believe our marriage is going to
work . . . without distractions on my part, anyway."
Oops, that had just slipped out. "Not that Hannah's
been distracted. I don't mean that. I . . . I . . ."

Robin's smile oozed with sympathy.

"I'm really tired, Robin," Marc said limply.

"Come lie down," she murmured, fluffing up the pillow beside her. "Mmmm. What's this?" Her hand came
out from under the pillow and she dangled between her
two fingers a gold-and-amber drop earring. "Unless this
is Hannah's, I see I've made my move too late."

Marc squinted from across the room. "What is it?"
He came nearer. And then suddenly his whole face lit
up. "It's Hannah's earring," he exclaimed, grabbing
Robin's wrist to examine the found object more closely.
"My God, it is. It's Hannah's earring. She was here. Last
night, she was here. She must have shown up after I
called home." Overcome with joy and relief, he pulled
Robin into his arms and hugged her. "Hannah slept here
last night. Right in this bed. Isn't that great? Isn't that

wonderful? She wasn't distracted. See. I knew it. I knew she wouldn't be. How could I have distrusted her even for a minute? From now on, I will trust Hannah implicitly."

Marc was so jubilant, he was completely oblivious to the new arrival standing in the open doorway of his bedroom. It was Robin Corbett who pointed out that they weren't alone. Prying herself from Marc's arms, Robin murmured, "Let's just hope, when the shoe's on the other foot, Hannah will feel the same way about you."

From the etched-in-granite look on Hannah's face at that moment, the odds were not in her husband's favor.

7

Family Ties

Hannah's apartment

"Were you really here all last night, Marc?"

"Every sleepless moment."

"And you really thought I was with another man?"

Marc smiled contritely. "Dumb. Dumb. Dumb."

Hannah raised a brow. "And Robin Corbett really means nothing to you?"

"Nothing. I explained all that. If Arnold Schwarzenegger was holding that earring of yours I would have hugged him."

Hannah frowned. "But she did proposition you."

Marc's smile deepened. "Let's just say it wasn't the kind of proposition that sets the pulse racing. She might as well have been proposing a business start-up plan."

Hannah held back for another moment and then threw her arms around her husband. "Our one chance in over a week to sleep together and we blew it. Worse, we doubted each other. Talk about dumb."

Marc rubbed Hannah's back. "We don't have to blow it tonight," he murmured against her ear.

Hannah sighed. "I promised Briskin I would go over a pile of reports tonight back at the office. I was supposed to stay after work to do them, but I was so tormented by my fantasies of where you'd spent the night...and then I thought about you and Robin alone tonight in your apartment . . . I told Briskin I had a personal emergency and I'd come back after dinner."

"Hannah, you work too hard."

"I know," Hannah said with a wry smile. "But Briskin's been on my case ever since we got married. He has this thing against married career women. He's sure the minute they say 'I do' they lose their ambition and drive. He's constantly testing me to see if I won't prove his theory correct."

Marc held her close. "He obviously doesn't know you."

Hannah nuzzled her head against Marc's shoulder. "Sometimes, I wonder if anyone really can have it all," she said in a low voice.

Marc cupped her chin and tilted her head up so that their eyes met. "You know what we need? We need to get away. My folks have been bugging me to bring you home to meet them. It'll be so relaxing spending a few quiet, unhassled days out in Minnesota. We can sleep late...."

"Sleep together."

"Take long walks...."

"And long breaks."

"Eat some real homemade pot roast...."

"Pot roast?"

"And fresh-from-the-oven apple pie."

Hannah smiled. "Mmmm. It does sound nice, Marc. And I would like to meet your family."

"Of course they'll make a fuss over you. But just at first."

Hannah drew away. "I am a little nervous about meeting them. They're so . . . traditional. They might think I'm—"

"We've been through this, Hannah. They'll think you're terrific. See, no hesitation before 'terrific.' Let's go, Hannah. We need this."

Hannah hesitated. "It'll be hard to get away. For both of us. We're so busy we hardly have time to breathe. Besides, Briskin will think he's scored a point for his theory if I ask for time off."

"The hell with Briskin and his theories."

"What about Ryder. How's he going to react?"

"The hell with Ryder," Marc said emphatically. "Neither one of us has taken a sick day or a personal day in two years. Well, I'm sick of not spending any personal time with you, Hannah. What do you say?"

Hannah touched Marc's cheek. He looked so earnest and young pleading his case. And even though she was nervous about meeting his family, the thought of spending a few quiet, tranquil days with Marc far away from all the stresses and hassles of the real world was too enticing to turn down. She smiled brightly. "I say . . . I do."

Marc pulled her tight to him and kissed her greedily. "Oh, Hannah, I love you."

She kissed him back. "I'm going to pretend last night was just a bad dream. We'll never doubt each other again. We'll be even more understanding, more supportive, more flexible."

"We won't let the ball drop. We'll just keep on juggling and we're bound to get better and better at it."

Hannah pulled Marc's shirt out from his trousers and let her fingers meander seductively up his back. "I think we've had that dreaded, oft talked about period of adjustment. It's going to be smooth sailing from here on in."

Marc cupped Hannah's face. "Do you really have to go back to work tonight?"

Hannah's face was flushed with arousal. "Yes...but, I did tell Briskin I'd have dinner first. How about having dinner with me? In bed?"

Marc's eyes sparkled. "Sure. That sounds wonderful. What are you in the mood for?"

Hannah smiled saucily. "Follow me and I'll show you."

"OH, THAT'S SO GOOD. Don't stop. Mmmm, that's so nice," Marc murmured as Hannah's lips cruised up and down his inner thigh, leaving tiny kisses along the trail.

"You are so tasty, Marc. If only we could dine like this every night," she whispered, moving up his body so that she was even with his face.

"That would be nice," he said, running a finger gently across her buttocks.

Hannah pressed herself against Marc more tightly, offering a brilliant, luminescent smile before devouring his mouth with hot, hungry kisses. At last she drew away and rolled off of him, sweat glistening on her body. "I'd like to stay here and make love with you all night," she sighed.

Marc nuzzled his face against her breasts. "No one ever accused me of being a slam, bam, thank you, ma'am sort of guy."

Hannah laughed. She'd told Marc about her friends' summation of the types of men that were available. "And you're not foolish, angry, or uncommitted. In fact, you're pretty damn terrific. How did I get so lucky?"

"I'm the lucky one," Marc insisted.

"I'm luckier."

Marc laughed. "Uh-uh, I am."

"No, no. Ask any of my friends. It is almost impossible to find a man who wants to share, communicate, make a lasting commitment to a relationship. Why do you think all those psychologists have to publish all those self-help books for women about finding and holding on to a man?"

"Your pal, Pam, seems to have read every one of them and I don't see how they helped her," Marc reflected.

"Which only proves my point about how tough it is to find a good man. So I win. I'm luckier."

Marc gave Hannah a rueful smile. "You really are a competitor, Hannah. But, in this case, I'll let it pass."

"You're so generous, Mr. Welles."

His hands began stroking her buttocks.

"Marc, don't. I really have to shower and get back to work."

"But, Hannah," Marc crooned, kissing the tip of her nose and then each eyelid, "you haven't had dessert."

"Oh, Marc, I can't...mmmmm, that's sinful... well, maybe a quick...piece of...something... sweet...for energy...."

Mondays, a restaurant on West 68th

HANNAH PULLED the mauve linen napkin shaped like a calla lily from her cut-glass goblet and spread it over her wool tweed skirt.

"So," she said, addressing her friends, "what's the special today?"

Diane grinned. "I hear it's the pig roast."

"Very funny," Hannah muttered.

"Stop teasing her, Diane," Pam interceded. "Can't you see the poor woman is a nervous wreck?"

"Well, it's no wonder," Laura declared. "She leaves for Minnesota tomorrow. I remember my first meeting with my in-laws. It was simply dreadful. Don's mother looked at me as if I were a wanton hussy who'd stolen off with her sweet, innocent baby boy. And his father... well, his father actually pinched my bottom when no one was looking. Of course, when I told Don, he told me it was my imagination. I told him it was his father who had the imagination."

"Please," Hannah pleaded. "I don't want to hear this. If Marc's father is a pincher I'll die."

"Oh, the pinch wasn't the worst part," Laura announced airily as her three cohorts' mouths all dropped open, their imaginations running riot for a moment. "The worst part of the visit was that Don's mother wouldn't let us sleep together."

"You and Don?" Diane asked facetiously.

"Of course, me and Don," Laura scolded.

"That's not that uncommon, actually," Pam said. "I was just reading the other day—"

"What was Don's mother's objection?" Hannah couldn't keep from asking. "You were married, after all."

"Not in her eyes. Don and I had a civil ceremony just like you and Marc. Don's mother declared that while the marriage might be legal in the eyes of the law, in her eyes and God's it was not."

"Oh, I'm sure Marc's mother won't feel that way," Hannah said, attempting a note of optimism in her voice, but failing. "Anyway, I'm not sure I'd really feel all that comfortable sleeping with Marc at his parents' home. It might be awkward."

"You'd be crazy to let a little awkwardness stop you," Pam said. "Let's face it, with you and Marc both being such workaholics and still not even living together, you guys haven't spent much time—"

"Please, Pam," Laura chided good-humoredly, "it's not polite to discuss such indelicate topics in a public restaurant."

Hannah sighed. "Pam is right. I went for my annual checkup yesterday and my doctor asked me if I were sexually active and I told her, I only wish."

"My doctor asked me that once," Diane said with a glint in her eye. "He was this really uptight, nervous sort. In this squeaky voice, he asks me if I'm sexually active, and I bat my eyelashes innocently at him and say, 'Oh, no, Dr. Shaw, I just lie there. I hardly move at all.' The poor man turned scarlet."

All the women laughed and the tight knot in Hannah's stomach loosened a little. After the waitress came over and took their orders, Hannah declared, "I'm really looking forward to this trip out to Minnesota.

Marc's told me his family is very warm and open, and I'm sure if I'm warm and open in return it'll work out just fine."

"Well, you'll know you're on solid ground," Laura said, "if Marc's mother doesn't have him bring his suitcase up to his old bedroom with its one single bed."

Arriving in Minnesota

AS THE PLANE STARTED to descend, Hannah gripped Marc's arm. "Oh Marc, I'm so nervous. Do you think they'll all be there waiting for us?"

"No, I don't think so. Just Mom and Dad. The rest of them will be waiting for us back home." Marc gently unpried Hannah's fingers from his wrist only to have her grab the sleeve of his jacket.

"What do I call them? I . . . I can't call them . . . Mom and Dad."

"Sure you can. They'd be tickled pink," Marc assured her.

"Do you think it's too late for the stewardess to get me a drink?"

"Hannah . . ."

"No, never mind. What would *Mom and Dad* think if they smelled liquor on my breath at eleven o'clock in the morning?"

Marc put his arm around Hannah and kissed her cheek. "Remember what I told you, darling. My folks are warm, open and affectionate. They'll take you right into their arms, and before you know it, you'll feel just like one of the family."

"What if I called them Mother and Father Welles?" Hannah obsessed. "Or...or Ma and Pa Welles? Or Jan and Bob?"

"Whatever you like, Hannah," Marc said soothingly.

Hannah folded her hands in her lap in an effort to relax. "Okay. Fine. I think Jan and Bob feels best." She tested it out. "Jan. Bob. How wonderful to meet you. Marc's told me such wonderful things about you both." She looked to her husband for his approval.

Marc smiled. "Good." He hesitated. "That's fine."

Hannah's hands sprang apart and she was once again making creases in Marc's jacket. "What? What is it? What's wrong?"

"Nothing's wrong. It's just . . ."

"Yes? Yes?"

"Well, you're meeting your in-laws, not doing a presentation where you've got to have the whole thing memorized. Maybe it would be better to just...say and do whatever comes into your mind when you meet them."

"But . . . what if nothing comes into my mind? What if my mind goes blank?"

Marc kissed her lightly on the lips. "Your mind has never gone blank, darling."

Hannah closed her eyes as the plane's landing wheels dropped. "Of course, there's still time for the plane to crash."

MARC GAVE HANNAH'S hand a squeeze as they entered the terminal. "Look, there they are." He waved broadly with his free hand.

"Where? Which ones are they?"

"Look, they spotted us. They're waving back."

"Oh, I see them." Hannah waved too. "They . . . they look nice. You look like your father. And your mom is sweet looking."

"See, I told you they didn't bite," Marc said, picking up his pace.

"Yes, but do they pinch?" Hannah muttered to herself, as Marc urged her on so that now she was walking just a couple of steps ahead of him. As they neared the large group clustered just outside the gated arrival area, Hannah made up her mind about her game plan. She'd go right up to Jan and Bob and give them both a big hug instead of waiting for them to make the first move. That would show them that she was a warm, affectionate woman, the perfect wife for their son. She moved more quickly, waving again to the small gray-haired woman and the tall, broad-shouldered man with the slight paunch. They looked just as she'd imagined them— cheerful, folksy, unpretentious, salt of the earth. And just look at how bright and welcoming their smiles were. Look how enthusiastically they waved. It was going to be all right, Hannah thought with relief. It was going to be more than all right.

"Mom. Dad. I'm so happy to be here," Hannah cried out, hugging first Mrs. Welles and then Mr. Welles. She was aware of the restraint of their responses, chalking it up to surprise at so spontaneous and affectionate a greeting from their new daughter-in-law. She didn't let that stop her. Curving her arm around *Mom's* shoulder, she smiled brightly in Marc's direction. "So, how does this son of yours look?"

Mom sputtered and Marc looked as red as a beet. Hannah frowned. Hadn't Marc encouraged her to be spontaneous, do what came naturally? Why was he looking so stunned? And why were his folks staring at her as if she were mad? And why was there this little group of onlookers gathering around her, staring at her in incredulity?

"Hannah." Marc turned even redder. "I'm ... uh ... afraid you've ... made a ... natural ... mistake."

The young woman holding a suitcase and standing beside Marc chuckled. "Yes, I'd say so."

"Mistake?" Hannah muttered.

Marc turned to his right where a tall, slender, middle-aged couple stood awkwardly observing the scene. "You see ... Hannah ... these are ... my parents."

"But ... but ..." Hannah still had her arm around *Mom* only now it turned out it wasn't *Mom* at all, at least not *her* mom. "But, you were waving right at me," the perplexed, mortified Hannah muttered inanely to the bewildered gray-haired woman.

"Well ... no, I was ... waving at my daughter," the woman explained shakily, gesturing to the young woman beside Marc. "She was right behind you."

"Oh," Hannah murmured weakly, only then realizing that she was still embracing this stranger who, very likely, thought she was a madwoman. Hannah quickly let her arm drop and stepped away. Now the blush on her face far surpassed Marc's. She stared at the man that she had taken to be Marc's father. "Marc ... doesn't really look that much like you ... after all."

As Hannah watched the young woman go off with *Mom and Dad*, all three of them laughing as soon as they got ten feet away, Hannah silently prayed that the floor would open up beneath her and she could just get swallowed up.

Marc and his parents stood awkwardly watching Hannah, none of them certain what to say or do. At the moment the folks that Marc had assured her were warm, friendly, affectionate people looked to Hannah like the somber, stoic pair of farmers from the painting, *American Gothic*.

"Hannah," Marc said finally, clearing his throat. "I'd like you to meet my parents. Mom, Dad, this is Hannah." He quirked a smile at his folks. "Isn't she terrific?"

Stiffly, Hannah extended her hand and as Marc's mother and father shook her hand in turn, Hannah eked out a greeting. "Mr. Welles. Mrs. Welles. I'm very pleased to meet you."

To Marc's parents' credit, they both smiled forgivingly at her, but Hannah could tell they were thinking that their sweet, innocent, wonderful son had married a bizarre nincompoop.

"Shall we go?" Marc's father said amiably.

As Marc's parents led the way through the terminal to the car, Hannah grimaced at Marc. "Next time, I'm sticking to the canned presentation, thank you."

The Welleses' home

HANNAH'S ANXIETY and humiliation had only heightened by the time Marc and his parents led her up the slate path to the cozy, two-story white-shingled farm-house. Mr. and Mrs. Welles's awkward silences during the forty-five-minute drive from the airport had only served to convince Hannah that this trip was a big mis-take. She should have waited, written to them for a while, gotten to know them via their letters, had them send along photographs.... Why hadn't she ever asked Marc to see any photos of his parents?

The front door sprang open and a pretty, fair-haired woman with a baby in each arm smiled cheerily as the small entourage started up the porch steps.

Hannah managed a weak smile back, but kept her arms glued to her sides.

"Susie," Marc called out, climbing the stairs two at a time. "You look too good to be the mother of twin babies."

"Oh, Marc, you sweet thing," Susie said, laughing. Then, as soon as they approached, she dumped one of the babies in Marc's arms, the other in Hannah's. "Hey, you two look good with twins."

Hannah, whose experience with babies was just about nil, held this tiny, wriggling bundle in her arms as if it was a time bomb about to go off at any moment.

"Now Susie," Mrs. Welles chided, taking the baby from Hannah as she urged them all into the house, "give Marc and Hannah a minute to breathe. They had a ... hectic ... arrival."

Hannah flushed scarlet, but Marc gave her an affec-tionate smile, handing the baby back to his sister. "We could use a bit of unwinding time."

"You'll have to unwind later," Susie said gaily. "You two didn't think the Welles family would let a wedding go uncelebrated."

"The wedding was almost three months ago," Marc said, taking Hannah's hand.

They were all in the hallway when the other celebrants sprang out of the living room, laughing and shouting their congratulations. To Hannah's dismay, they all converged around her and Marc, tossing off introductions and embraces and well-wishes. There was Susie's husband, Len, Alicia, Roy, and their three children, Marc's older brother, Gordon, who looked incredibly like a heavier version of Marc, several aunts, uncles and cousins. And, to Hannah's horror, there was even a minister present. Hannah's panic soared. Could Marc's parents have disapproved of their civil ceremony and be planning a second wedding? Hannah was still getting over the trauma of the first one. She was definitely not prepared for another. Dr. Rusman's final chapter of his latest bestseller sprang unbidden into her mind. "I do. Do I?"

The minister turned out to be a next-door neighbor who'd simply come over to join in the festivities, which involved a big buffet dinner and a huge, home-baked, three-tiered wedding cake with the requisite white icing and the bride and groom figurines on top. Ending the festivities was the opening of a tableload of wedding gifts.

There were several toaster ovens, food processors, blenders, juicers and mixers. Marc's sister Alicia had bought them a set of towels with the initials *MW&HW.* Hannah decided this was probably not the best time to explain she'd kept her maiden name and therefore her maiden initials.

Besides the lavish set of sterling silver flatware Marc's parents gave them, Mrs. Welles had a special gift for Hannah.

When Hannah first unwrapped the present she thought it was a diary. But then she opened the cloth-covered book and saw that there were hand-printed recipes inside.

"All of Marc's favorites," Mrs. Welles said with a tender smile. "And from the look of him, my dear, I'd say he could do with some ample servings of home-cooked food." Mrs. Welles had indexed the recipes covering everything from soups to desserts. She sat down next to Hannah and pointed out one after another of his childhood favorites.

"Of course, some of these recipes are a bit tricky," Mrs. Welles said, pausing at one entitled Momma's Moist and Marvelous Chicken n' Dumplings. "But with a little practice you'll get the knack."

Since Hannah had barely achieved the knack of boiling water, her smile was less than optimistic. Not to mention the fact that her marriage was not founded on the little woman spending her days merrily sweating over a hot stove, preparing her husband's favorite recipes. If Marc wanted a favorite recipe, he'd have to track down a restaurant that served it. And chances were fifty-fifty, he'd be enjoying his feast alone.

Marc grinned at her, and Hannah was certain he knew what she was thinking, but thankfully he didn't say anything.

"Open mine next," Susie prodded.

Hannah was only too happy to set Momma's recipe book aside.

Susie's gift was an exquisite antique silver frame.

"For your wedding picture," Susie said. "Every couple should have a special frame for their favorite wedding picture."

"Oh, well, we don't actually have a wedding picture," Marc said, not quite meeting his sister's eye.

"Oh, you must," his mother exclaimed. "Why, every bride and groom must have a wedding photo."

"I've got a great idea," Alicia, Marc's older sister exclaimed, jumping up from the couch. "Roy's got his camera here. And Mom, don't you still have my wedding dress put away in the cedar closet upstairs?"

"And Dad, you've got that old tux you wore when you and Mom renewed your vows three years ago," Gordon added. "It should do nicely for Marc."

Jan Welles seemed thrilled with the idea of a wedding dress-up. She was so enthusiastic, Hannah didn't have the heart to protest. Instead, she just gave Mom a wilted smile and let Alicia and Susie drag her upstairs to help her change. So, she hadn't been spared a wedding after all.

"GO ON, MARC, feed her a piece of cake," Alicia urged. "You've got to have a cake-eating picture for your wedding album.

"Oops, Hannah, you might want to wipe that piece of icing off your nose," Susie suggested.

"Look natural," Mom instructed.

"Smile," ordered Roy as he clicked.

"Okay, now the garter toss," Susie announced.

Hannah gave Marc a *must I* look and he smiled encouragingly. Hannah pulled up her dress, awkwardly stepped out of the borrowed garter and tossed it. Alicia's oldest boy, Bradley, caught it and immediately stuck it on his head.

"That's a wrap," Roy said.

Hannah would have breathed a sigh of relief if she could. Unfortunately Alicia's wedding dress was a size eight, and Hannah wore a ten. If she breathed she'd surely rip a seam.

After the aunts, uncles and neighbors took off and Hannah and Marc had changed into their civvies again, they came downstairs to find the women sorting through the gifts, the men having gone off to the den to watch a basketball game on the TV.

"Dear me," Marc's mother said to them as they entered the room, "you've got so many duplicates. What will you do with two food processors, two toaster ovens . . . ?"

"Actually, for the time being," Marc said offhandedly, "Hannah can keep one in her place and I can keep one in mine."

"What?" his mother gasped. Alicia and Susie gave Marc and Hannah puzzled looks.

"We're looking for an apartment for the two of us," Hannah said in a rush. "Finding a decent place in midtown Manhattan is like finding a needle in a haystack."

"You haven't set up house yet?" Marc's mother said, still not quite taking it in.

"Well, that's certainly a modern marriage you have there," Susie chirped. "I guess there's always room for . . . variety."

Alicia frowned. "I don't know why the two of you want to settle in New York City, anyway. There are plenty of opportunities for you, Marc, over in Minneapolis. It's a nice, safe, clean city, a good environment for raising a family."

"We love Manhattan," Hannah said, more sharply than she'd intended.

"Besides, Hannah and I both have terrific jobs in the city, with lots of potential for growth. For both of us," Marc emphasized.

Hannah pressed her hands together. Her palms were sweaty. "Marc's very supportive . . . of my career."

"And what about the children?" Marc's mother queried.

Hannah's brow creased. "What children?"

"You do plan to have children, don't you?" Alicia asked.

Susie smiled. "Beware. Twins run in the family."

Hannah's throat went dry. "I'm sure we will have a child once we're both where we want to be in our careers."

"And after the child?" Marc's mother persisted.

"Just think, if you lived closer to home," Alicia pointed out before Hannah could respond to Mrs. Welles's question, "you'd have three built-in babysitters—Mom, Susie and me. That is, if you wanted to work part-time after the baby, Hannah. Lots of women do, although personally, I don't know how they manage it. I guess they've got a different breed of husband, one that's willing to pitch in doing housework and cooking and the like. That's not Roy, and if you're thinking that's Marc, well, all I can tell you is Mom never could get that boy to tidy up his room or help with the supper, or anything like that."

"I'm sure if . . . when . . . we have a child, Marc and I will share equally in the responsibilities of child care and the house," Hannah said stiffly.

"Sure," Marc said, his voice huskier than usual. "Plenty of wives and mothers are career women."

"And what do these career women do with their babies when they're off at their careers?" Marc's mother inquired archly.

Marc looked to Hannah and she replied, "There are many excellent child-care facilities in Manhattan."

There was a tense silence. The bubbly Susie came to the rescue. "I don't see why we're even having this discussion at this point. These two are still newlyweds. And everyone knows newlyweds have all sort of notions about what married life is going to be like. We have no right to disillusion them."

Alicia laughed. "True. They'll find out the hard, bitter facts of life soon enough on their own."

Susie put an affectionate arm around Hannah. "You look beat. I think you and Marc ought to go right upstairs and get yourselves a good night's sleep."

Marc's mother rose from the sofa. "Yes, of course, you both must be exhausted. Go ahead. The girls will help me tidy up."

Marc smiled with relief. He was only too happy to get off behind a closed door alone with his wife. Hannah was equally eager.

"You'll take Dad's and my room, Marc," Mrs. Welles called out.

Hannah stopped dead in her tracks. Here she was worried about Marc's parents wanting them to sleep in separate rooms, and instead, but even more unnerving, they were putting them up in the master bedroom.

Marc was no more happy with the arrangement than Hannah. It was just too awkward. "Don't be silly, Mom. We'll take the spare room. It's got the foldout couch."

"Not anymore it doesn't. We redecorated and made it into my sewing room."

"Well, then my old room."

"Nonsense. Bunk beds? I wouldn't hear of it," his mother insisted.

"But, where will you sleep?" Hannah asked Mrs. Welles.

"Why, we'll sleep right here on the living-room sofa bed."

"No," Hannah insisted, "Marc and I can sleep here. We couldn't put you out of your own room."

"Why, there's absolutely no privacy down here. Dad and I are up at the crack of dawn, so it's just as well for us. But, surely, you wouldn't want us tromping around about you, while the two of you were trying to sleep in. When Marc called to tell us your arrival time, he mentioned how much the two of you were looking forward to sleeping late and relaxing. Now, upstairs, both of you. And I don't want to hear another word."

"MARC? ARE YOU still awake?"

"Yes."

"Do you feel as weird as I do sleeping in your parents' bed?"

"Weirder."

"Do you think we haven't quite finished with that period of adjustment?"

"Definitely."

8

Setting Up House

439 Park Avenue between 62nd and 63rd

HANNAH AND MARC stood in the center of the empty living room, Hannah's mother hovering close by.

"So?" Mary Logan asked anxiously. "Is it perfect or is it perfect?"

Hannah looked at Marc. Marc looked at Hannah. They each cocked an eyebrow. Then slowly, in unison, they looked at Mary.

"Perfect," they said together.

Mary Logan let out the whoosh of air she'd been holding expectantly in her lungs. She could hardly believe their response. She'd only dragged either one or both of them to at least two dozen other possibilities, none of which, it seemed, was anything close to perfect. Mary was getting worried that her daughter and son-in-law would never actually set up house. And that, thought Mary Logan, spelled big trouble. It was her opinion that there was just so much apartness a marriage could withstand.

Mary eyed them cautiously. "You mean it? You love it? You'll take it?"

Hannah gave her mother a hug. "We mean it. We love it. We'll take it."

Mary looked to Marc for confirmation. He smiled broadly at his mother-in-law. "I bet you were beginning to think we'd never find a place we liked."

Mary grinned. "The thought had crossed my mind." She picked up her raincoat. "Well, I'll leave the two of you to handle the technicalities." She gave the large, airy living room with its cozy dining nook and marble fireplace one last survey. "Oh, won't it be fun for the two of you to decorate this place? Victorian would go beautifully, but of course the two of you have your own preferences."

"I suppose," Hannah said, giving Marc a thoughtful look.

"I figured I'd leave the decorating to you, Hannah," Marc said.

"How do I fit decorating a six-room apartment into my schedule?" Hannah queried.

"Well, for now we can just move the stuff over from both our apartments. One of us can take the larger bedroom and use it as a combination sleeping space and office. The other can use the two smaller rooms," Marc suggested.

Mary Logan, who was about to exit the living room, stopped dead in her tracks, spun around and gave them both an incredulous shake of the head. "I know it's terribly traditional, but don't even the most modern of couples usually share a bedroom?"

Hannah smiled. "Well, of course, we'll consider the larger bedroom the master bedroom for all intents and purposes. It's just that Marc and I are used to a certain degree of privacy. We both have different work schedules, and Marc likes to get to bed earlier so he can wake up and do some work at the crack of dawn. . . ."

"And Hannah comes alive at midnight just when I'm ready to hit the hay."

"Right. I get my best work done at one, two in the morning," Hannah explained.

Mary Logan sighed. "Well, personally, I'm old-fashioned. I think the couple that goes to bed together, stays wed together."

"Not to be rude, Mother," Hannah said gently, "but that little proverb of yours didn't exactly keep your marriage together."

"Or six out of every ten other marriages," Marc added. "The way Hannah and I see it, most couples start coming unglued after marriage because they feel obliged to turn their previously well-ordered, comfortable, unpressured lives upside-down in a misguided effort to accommodate their mate. Which, of course, is doomed to failure, which leads to disappointments, with one or the other feeling wronged."

"Right," Hannah was quick to affirm. "You hear it all the time. The wife complains that the husband is never home on time for dinner—"

"And the husband complains that the wife hasn't made his dinner—"

"Or she's in a snit because he doesn't help enough around the house, or he spends more free time with his business associates than he does with her, or he's not romantic anymore, or—"

Marc quickly picked up the ball. "Or she's too independent and doesn't make him feel needed, or she's too aggressive, or she isn't nurturing enough. . . ."

Hannah walked over to her mother and put her arm around her shoulder. "You see, Mother, Marc and I don't want to make the same mistakes as...as so many other people have made. We want to do it right."

"Yes," Marc agreed. "We want this marriage to last."

"And if we just follow our plan," Hannah added, almost a bit too emphatically, "we'll do . . . just fine."

"Yes," Marc said, nodding his head. "Just fine."

Mary Logan held her hands up in surrender. "Okay, maybe you've got the right idea. God knows the rest of us certainly seem to be at a loss in this game. If it works for you children, then all I can say is . . ." She stopped, giving them both a pitying look. "All I can say is marriage has become a rather dreary, colorless business. Personally, I think I'd rather do it all wrong, and at least have some fun, passion, and excitement along the way."

After Mary Logan left the vacant apartment, leaving Hannah and Marc alone, a distinct pall hung in the air, as did the echo of Mary Logan's parting remark. Hannah and Marc strolled the empty rooms together, making strained remarks about where they'd put their desks, their computers, fax machines, the beds and bureaus. Finally, in the middle of what was meant to be the master bedroom, Hannah turned to Marc, a hint of desperation shadowing her features.

"We have fun, passion and excitement in our marriage, don't we, Marc?"

To Hannah's dismay, Marc's affirmative response wasn't exactly forthcoming. And when it did come, it wasn't exactly emphatic. "I think we have...our share. I mean . . . it takes some juggling."

Hannah was beginning to hate that word. "But, you don't feel that our marriage is . . . dreary . . . colorless?"

A muscle jumped in Marc's jaw. "Do you?"

Hannah felt a sudden rush of tears threatening. "We knew it wouldn't be easy. Now . . . now that we've got our own place . . . well . . ." She swallowed hard, then gripped Marc's suit jacket. There was a quality of desperation in her grasp. "Let's make love, Marc. Remember that afternoon we made love in that vacant apartment? I bet Mother never had an afternoon that passionate and exciting . . . that much fun." She began wrenching the jacket off his shoulders, forgetting to unbutton it.

"Hannah, we can't. Not . . . now," Marc protested softly. "I've got a 2:15 appointment over in Jersey and you told me you had to be back by one for a staff meeting."

Hannah was pulling at his tie. "Oh, Marc . . ."

"Come on, Hannah. You know you'll hate yourself later if you don't show up on time for that staff meeting. Especially now that you're trying so hard to convince Briskin that you're his best bet for that promotion to development you want so badly."

She had the loop of Marc's paisley tie halfway over his head. She let it slide back down over his face and then she collapsed against him. "You're right."

Hannah's acquiescence to common sense ironically sparked Marc's desire to throw appointments, meetings and promotions to the wind. His hands glided seductively down Hannah's back. "On the other hand, it has been a while, Hannah. And sometimes being right isn't all that much fun." His hands cruised over her buttocks as he pressed her tighter to him.

"No, Marc," Hannah protested, albeit weakly, "we should be sensible...practical...responsible." She looked up all misty-eyed at him. "Shouldn't we?"

"I...suppose," he murmured, but his eyes said *the hell with responsibility.*

Hannah's fingers were already working on Marc's fly as she slithered down to her knees. "I want you, Marc. I want to be wild and wanton with you. I want to show them all...."

Marc swayed a little and had to grip Hannah's shoulders for support. "Oh, yes...yes, my wild, wanton witch...."

At first Hannah thought the ringing sound she was hearing was the proverbial bells one is supposed to hear when one is madly in love.

"Hannah."

"Mmmm."

"Isn't that a...phone?"

"We don't have...a phone...yet, darling."

"I think...it's definitely...a phone," he murmured breathlessly.

Hannah sat abruptly back on her heels. "Damn. It's my cellular phone. I stuck it in my briefcase." She looked wanly up at him. "I...I better answer it, darling. I've got this...deal in the works."

"Oh...right..."

"Don't go away," she whispered. "I'll be right back." She winked before scooting out of the room. "I never leave a project hanging."

Ten minutes later, Marc popped his head into the living room where Hannah was sitting yoga style on the floor, still talking on the phone.

"I know Rollins wants to target the downtown Denver area first, but like I said in my report, it still requires a redo of the traffic pattern. We've got to develop a more effective strategy before—" she looked across at Marc and gave him a sad, apologetic shrug "—before he ends up creating even more congestion."

Marc gave Hannah a wistful but understanding smile. He straightened his tie, made sure he was all in tidy order, picked up his own briefcase and gave Hannah a little wave.

"Yes, yes, I know all that, but . . ." She waved glumly back at Marc and continued talking as she watched him leave the apartment. As she heard the front door click shut, she felt an overwhelming, inexplicable sense of loss. "Do you honestly think it makes sense for me to go flying off to Denver for two weeks to hold his hand . . . ? You do . . . Tomorrow. Right." Hannah blinked back threatening tears. "Yes, yes, I know where you're coming from. . . ." A few errant tears went trickling down Hannah's cheeks. "No, no, I don't want you to send anyone else." The tears were running rampant now. "No, I'm fine. Just . . . a little . . . cold. Nothing . . . serious. I'll . . . get over it. . . ."

"OH, HANNAH, RELAX. You've been wound tight since you got back from Denver. Following a recipe shouldn't be all that stressful," Pam said as she watched Hannah frantically pour over Momma Welles's Meat n' Tater Pie recipe.

"I've never made a meal for Marc before. Not a *real* meal." She frowned as she continued studying the recipe. "I went through every recipe in this damn book Marc's mother gave me of all his favorite meals and this one seemed the least complicated." She looked wanly up at Pam. "Which is not saying much. What's a roux, do you think?"

Pam shrugged. "You're asking me? I burn water."

Hannah slammed the book shut. "I can't do this. I can't do this, Pam."

"You can tell Marc you thought about doing it. It's the thought that counts. Besides, Marc doesn't expect you to cook for him."

"That's why I wanted to do it. I wanted to do something unexpected, different. I felt like such a heel taking off for Denver for two weeks, leaving Marc to cope with getting all our stuff moved into this place by himself. He didn't even complain. I wanted to do something to show him how much I appreciate him."

"You're so lucky, Hannah. Marc is so incredibly understanding and supportive."

"I know."

"Not that you don't give as good as you get."

"I try my best."

"And it's working." Pam grinned. "So maybe Dr. Rusman doesn't have all the answers. Maybe you and Marc ought to write the definitive book on a successful two-career marriage."

Hannah smiled facetiously. "Right. I could call it *The Two-Career Marriage Guide To Parallel Parking.* We'll do it in our spare time.

"I've got to admit," Pam said, giving Hannah a reflective look, "we all had our doubts about the two of you for a while. We honestly didn't think this business-plan marriage of yours would really work. We were sure you'd never be able to pull it off."

Hannah's smile quirked on and off briefly. "Well, it isn't as if there aren't any . . . kinks, of course. After all, even the most thought-out plans, once they're put into operation, can show . . . flaws."

"Flaws?" Pam raised an eyebrow. "What flaws? You told me the two of you just about never argue, there are no apparent conflicts, you're both incredibly understanding and supportive. Honey, it doesn't get much better."

"I . . . I suppose you're right," Hannah muttered, abruptly turning back to Mother Welles's recipe book, studying the page with a vengeance. "Could a meat n' tater pie really be all that difficult for a woman with an MBA?"

Pam grinned. "Not to mention a woman who just landed a promotion to head of team development."

Hannah smiled. "I never thought Briskin would come through on that. I guess he was really impressed with my work out in Denver."

"Denver was the icing on the cake. You've proved yourself time and again. Let's face it, Hannah, you finally convinced him marriage was not going to interfere with your career."

Hannah was staring down at the recipe, but her vision was blurred as she murmured in a low, dry voice, "Yes, I convinced him, all right." While she tried hard to focus on the instructions for the meat n' tater pie, she was distressed and confused by these odd pangs of self-pity that seemed to sneak up on her at the most unexpected moments. Several nights in her hotel room in Denver she'd actually cried herself to sleep. That wasn't like her. She tried to tell herself it was just the typical pressures of work, refusing to acknowledge that her marriage was adding any additional strain. On the face of it, it wasn't. As Pam implied, she and Marc had an ideal marriage. So why was she having these crying jags? Why, if their plan was working so well, was she so moody lately? Why was she feeling so desperate?

"I've got to make this recipe," Hannah said so emphatically that Pam laughed.

"Well, Hannah, every time you put your mind to something, you usually succeed." Pam reached for her light wool blazer, which she'd tossed on the back of her chair.

"Where are you going?" There was a panic in Hannah's voice.

"Home. Believe it or not, I've actually got a date tonight."

"Oh, Pam, can't you just stay until I put this concoction together? I need moral support."

Pam slipped on her jacket. "I break out in hives if I hang around a kitchen too long. It's hard enough playing the dating game if you look halfway decent. With hives, I can forget ever finding Mr. Right."

Hannah sighed dramatically. "Okay, okay. Go. Desert me. Leave me in my time of need."

Pam grinned as she headed for the door. "If it comes out edible bring me in some of the leftovers for my lunch tomorrow."

"No sirree. You don't reap the rewards unless you put in the work," Hannah shouted as Pam made her retreat.

"Great," Hannah muttered as she returned to her task.

A half hour later, as the food processor was spitting out huge chunks of mashed potato all over Hannah and the kitchen counter, the phone rang. It was Hannah's mother.

"Oh, thank God it's you, Mother."

"Hannah, what is it? Are you ill? You sound dreadful."

"It's the damn food processor. I think it's an alien from outer space in disguise."

"The food processor? What are you doing with the food processor?"

"Well, that's a pretty foolish question. What does one usually do with a food processor? I'm processing food. Potatoes, to be exact. But, for every potato I toss into the infernal machine it manages to spit out a good two."

"That's impossible. Unless you forgot to put the...the doohickey in the lid."

"The doohickey? What doohickey?"

"The plunger piece. For heaven's sake, Hannah. It fits right into the feeder cavity. For such a successful businesswoman who runs complex computers, fax machines and the like, I'd have thought you'd have no difficulty running a food processor. Didn't you even read the manual?"

Hannah bent down and pulled the carton out from the cabinet. She found the instruction manual and the missing part. "I naively thought there'd be nothing to it," Hannah admitted.

"Homemaking is not a snap, my dear. And since when did you decide to cook real mashed potatoes, Hannah?"

"Since I decided that, for a change, I'd surprise Marc with a decent home-cooked meal, that's when. I'm . . . uh . . . whipping up a meat n' tater pie, which is one of Marc's favorites. Well, at this point, it's going to be more meat than tater."

"Why Hannah, how domestic."

"Yes, well, I thought it might be . . . fun. I've got the dining table set with the china you gave us, the flatware from Marc's parents, and the crystal goblets the girls at Unicom gave us."

"Candles?"

"Of course."

"Sounds romantic, darling."

"Yes, it does, doesn't it?" Hannah said with a smile, thinking about the little number she planned to wear for her romantic dinner with her husband.

"Well, I won't keep you then. Don't forget about sticking that doohickey into that hole now."

Hannah stared wide-eyed at the receiver. "What did you say, Mother?"

"In your food processor, darling. Before you do any more whipping."

"Oh, I won't," Hannah said, giggling as she hung up. "I won't."

An hour later, the meat n' tater pie safely ensconced in the oven, Hannah was gleefully getting ready. With a lusty smile, she opened the box containing her new purchase, an absolutely sinful lace and satin black teddy. That and a little blush was all she planned to wear to greet her husband. If this didn't put him in a romantic mood, nothing would.

Slipping on the sexy and very skimpy item of underwear, Hannah felt a rush of arousal. She began singing, "Tonight's the night . . ." as she practiced one seductive pose after another in her mirror. Then, she checked the bedside clock radio. Eight-fifteen. She frowned. She'd called Marc's office at seven and the secretary said he was just finishing up and should be on his way within the hour. She considered calling again, but then decided he must have left. Instead, she hurried back into the kitchen and turned the oven down a bit.

By eight forty-five, Hannah decided to phone CSR. No answer. Great, Marc was on his way. As she gave the meat n' tater pie in the oven another check, she frowned. It was getting kind of dried-out looking. What could she expect? She had cooked it over a half hour longer than the recipe called for. But she kept thinking Marc would walk in at any moment, and she wanted him to smell that long-forgotten scent of an old familiar favorite. Hannah smiled. She did feel quite domestic. It didn't feel bad.

It was ten after nine when Hannah heard the key turn in the front door. Forgetting her mounting irritation at Marc's late arrival, she frantically lit the candles on the table, turned on the CD player so that lush strings filled the room and posed herself seductively on the sofa.

"Hannah, I'm home," Marc called out.

She didn't answer. Let him be surprised. Her position got a little more seductive.

"Hannah? Hey, what's that weird smell?"

The lights flicked on in the living room, revealing Hannah in all her almost naked glory. It also revealed Marc . . . and a tall, well-dressed stranger.

Hannah gasped in shock and mortification. Marc and the man beside him were pretty flabbergasted themselves.

"Hannah?"

In desperation, Hannah rolled off the couch hitting her head on the edge of the coffee table as she propelled herself under it. She let out a sharp cry of pain mingled with a hefty dose of rage and humiliation. To make matters worse, the coffee table had a clear glass top.

The man with Marc did have the decency, after regaining his wits, to discreetly exit the room as Marc rushed to Hannah's aid.

"Hannah, you're hurt," he said with alarm, bending down on his hands and knees.

"How could you do this? How could you . . . Who is that man?"

"Elliot Bloomenthal. I . . . I thought we'd stop by the apartment to see if you wanted to join us for dinner. He wanted to meet you."

"Bloomenthal? Bloomenthal." The same Bloomenthal whom she'd had a nightmare about on the night Marc showed up late for their honeymoon. In her dream he'd looked like the book-cover photo of Dr. Rusman. In real life he was a tall, attractive man in his mid-forties. "Well, he met me all right," she moaned.

"Hannah, let me look at your head. You really whacked it. You might have gotten a concussion."

"I couldn't be that lucky," she muttered.

"What are you . . . dressed like that for?" he whispered, baffled. "And what's that terrible smell?"

Forgetting the throbbing pain and the growing lump on her head, she crawled out from under the table and glared at him. "That smell is your old favorite, meat n' tater pie. Just like your mother used to make. And I was dressed like this because . . . because . . . I had suffered a momentary mental breakdown," she shouted as she stormed off to her room and slammed the door.

Marc started after her, but the door was locked by the time he got to it. "Hannah . . ."

"Go away. Go take Bloomenthal to dinner."

Marc had almost forgotten about his important client. What must the poor man be thinking out there in the foyer? "Hannah," Marc whispered, "why don't you throw something on and we'll eat that meat n' tater pie. It . . . smells . . . delicious."

"Go away."

Elliot Bloomenthal popped his head into the living room. He motioned to Marc. Distraught and embarrassed, Marc joined his client in the foyer.

"I'm really sorry, Elliot. Hannah doesn't usually . . . She isn't . . . I never expected . . ."

Elliot Bloomenthal grinned. "Hey, you've got nothing to apologize for. If I could have a wife who greeted me the way your wife greets you after a hard day at the office, I'd consider marriage myself. Why don't we take a rain check on that dinner and you and your wife enjoy that home-cooked meal she prepared for you?"

Marc gave Bloomenthal a dazed look. "I can't believe Hannah did that. She's never cooked anything but
a hamburger before."

Bloomenthal's grin deepened. "If you want a piece
of friendly advice, Marc, whatever it tastes like, tell her
it's delicious. Better than anything your mother ever
made."

"Right," Marc said with an earnest smile.

HANNAH, THIS PIE IS . . . great. I can't . . . believe how
good . . . it is. Better than Mom's."

"It is not good. It's awful. There aren't enough potatoes, the meat got overcooked, it smells burnt."

"It's not true. Please unlock the door and come out
and taste some yourself."

"How could you have brought a client home like that
without even letting me know?"

"How was I to know you'd chosen this particular
night to . . . to . . . greet me in your underwear?"

"I wanted it to be a surprise."

"It was a surprise."

"I wanted it to be romantic. Exciting. Passionate. Instead, it's turned out to be the singularly most embarrassing moment of my life."

"Come on, Hannah, if anything, you helped me score
some points with Bloomenthal. He thought I was damn
lucky to have a wife like you."

"You don't have a wife like me. He only thinks you
do. I'm not really a wife at all. At least I don't feel particularly like a wife."

"What do you feel like?"

"I feel . . . like a total failure."

"Oh, Hannah, you've never failed at anything. We just got our signals crossed. Open the door, darling. We can still have fun, excitement, passion. . . ."

"No, the mood is gone, Marc." She unlocked the door and opened it. Marc gasped in alarm as he saw that the lump on Hannah's forehead now closely resembled the proverbial golf ball.

Instead of spending the night locked in passionate embrace with her husband in their rarely shared queen-size bed in the master bedroom, Hannah spent a miserable night under observation in a hospital bed at the General.

All in all, as their marriage had been going, it seemed to Hannah par for the course.

9

The Seven-Month Itch

Romeo's, an Italian café on 83rd

"HANNAH, YOU HAVEN'T eaten a thing," Laura commented, spearing her last artichoke heart from her antichpasto. "Are you okay?"

"Fine," Hannah said weakly.

"It isn't still your head, is it?" Pam asked solicitously, even though it had been close to three weeks since Hannah had ended up in the hospital with a mild concussion.

"No," Hannah said. "My head is fine." Hannah had told the group about her accidental collision with the coffee table, but she'd been too embarrassed to tell them the details leading up to it.

Diane bit off a piece of bread stick and waved the rest of it at Hannah, giving her a scrutinizing study. "You aren't pregnant, are you?"

Hannah laughed dryly. "Not unless it's an immaculate conception."

Pam gave her friend a sympathetic smile and then turned to the others. "Marc's been out of town for the past couple of weeks. And before that Hannah was recuperating from her concussion. And before that she was out in Denver." She turned back to Hannah. "Too bad the two of you can't seem to coordinate your schedules so that you can both be on business trips at the same time."

"I'll mention that to Briskin." Hannah made an effort to swallow a bit of her veal scallopini.

Laura sighed. "Well, talking about pregnancy, I've decided I'd like to have a baby. As much as I hate the phrase, my biological clock is ticking."

"Nonsense," Diane snickered. "You haven't even hit thirty. Your clock's barely wound up."

Pam dabbed her mouth with her napkin. "I just finished Porter's book, *Women, Wombs, and Work,*, and he did this study that showed career women who had their children in their late twenties rather than their late thirties, were actually better able to combine their work and family life because they had more energy, they were more flexible."

"The hell with work," Laura said, helping herself to a taste of Hannah's veal. "I don't see what the great shakes is in being superwoman. So, you have it all. Do you have any time to enjoy it?"

Laura's eyes rested on Hannah. "Not much," Hannah admitted.

"Precisely," Laura replied. "I tell you, ladies, if I could find a warm, loving, successful man who could take care of me, I'd gladly give up my quest for self-sufficiency, self-reliance and independence. So, string me up."

Diane finished her bread stick. "And where do you expect to find this knight in shining armor?"

Laura's eyes twinkled and she leaned forward conspiratorially. "Well, ladies, there happens to be a divine figure of a man sitting a few tables over, who keeps looking this way. He could be the one."

Diane raised a brow. "Which one of us is he eyeing?"

Laura shrugged. "I can't tell."

Pam sat up a little straighter and tried to peek without being too obvious. "The sandy blonde with the mustache?"

"No. Two tables to his right. Dark hair, blue suit, power tie, sitting with a paunchy, gray-haired man."

"Mmmm," Diane murmured, taking a quick, surreptitious look. "Not bad. And you're right, he does seem interested in someone at our table."

"If he's interested in me, he's probably married," Pam muttered, also giving the attractive diner a quick check. "For some reason I seem to draw married men like flypaper draws flies. Only the flies stick."

Laura sighed, giving the diner across the way a more overt study. "That gorgeous man and I could make lovely babies."

"The suit is definitely custom," Diane said, brow arched. "That's a good sign."

"And he's got excellent table manners," Pam added, managing another glimpse out of the corner of her eye. "I love a man who can twirl his pasta so expertly. Fine finger coordination is a big plus in my book."

Hannah laughed. "Ladies, ladies. Aren't you all acting a bit desperate?"

"Who's acting?" Laura quipped.

"All right, where is the dreamboat sitting?" Hannah asked, her curiosity finally peaked.

"Drop your napkin on the floor, and then, when you bend to pick it up, glance straight behind you two tables. You can't miss him," Laura said.

Hannah felt a little silly, but she crossed her legs so that the napkin on her lap slid off. She kicked it back with her heel so that she had a better excuse to turn. She swiveled in her seat and, as she started to bend down for the napkin, she looked over at this man who inspired such lust in her friends. At the precise moment she spotted him, he looked her way. For an instant their eyes locked and the man smiled at her. It was one of those Cartier smiles—sparkling and luxurious.

Hannah's response was less than beguiling. Her mouth fell open as recognition dawned. She quickly spun around, forgetting all about the napkin.

"Well?" Laura queried. "Is he the perfect father for my baby or what?"

Diane gave Hannah a quizzical gander. "You look like you've seen a ghost, not a dreamboat. What's the matter?"

Before Hannah could respond, Pam said breathlessly, "Oh, God, he's coming over here."

Laura quickly fluffed her hair. "Mmmm. Give me a take-charge man any time."

Hannah's eyes darted to the exit. Would it seem too weird if she leapt out of her chair and made a run for it? Uh-oh, too late.

"Well, hello, Mrs. Welles. I wasn't sure at first it was you. You look different dressed in your...work clothes." The man's deep blue eyes sparkled.

Pam, Laura and Diane all wore expressions that combined drooling envy with abject curiosity as Hannah gave the man standing beside her chair a wilted smile. "Hello, Mr. Bloomenthal."

"Elliot, please."

Hannah could feel the redness heating up her cheeks. At the same time she had to remember that, as embarrassing as it was to come face-to-face with Bloomenthal again after that encounter in which he'd come face-to-face with most of her body, he was one of her husband's most important clients.

"Mr. Bloom . . . Elliot, these are my . . . colleagues." Somehow, she managed the introductions. The three women beamed, but it was obvious to all of them that Mr. Elliot Bloomenthal only had eyes for Hannah. From the expressions on their faces, it was obvious they found it decidedly unfair.

After the intros Elliot Bloomenthal focused his full attention back on Hannah. "How are you feeling now? I learned from Marc that you ended up with a concussion."

"Mild," Hannah muttered, growing redder by the moment. "A mild concussion."

Bloomenthal's hand touched her shoulder. "I hope you don't hold it against me."

Hannah could feel her friends' eyes boring into her. Curiouser and curiouser.

"No," she blurted. "Of course not."

Bloomenthal glanced down at Hannah's plate of barely touched veal scallopini. "I see you didn't care for the food here any more than I did. I happen to know a spot on the lower east side that does incredible things with veal. Maybe you and your husband will let me take you there one evening this week for dinner. I'll be in town until Friday. How about tomorrow night?"

Hannah couldn't decide which she found more unnerving, Elliot Bloomenthal's piercing blue eyes or her friends' gaping stares. "I'm afraid...Marc won't be back until . . . Saturday. He's in . . . Pittsburgh."

"Oh. Pittsburgh. That's too bad. I was hoping to see him."

"Yes. Well . . . he's in Pittsburgh. Till Saturday," Hannah repeated inanely, wishing those dancing blue eyes of Mr. Elliot Bloomenthal would stop dancing in her direction. She felt this strong compulsion to blurt out something even more inane, like *Please Mr. Bloomenthal, I'm a married woman. My dancing days are over.*

439 Park Avenue

HANNAH DUMPED HER TOTE BAG, the pile of mail and her take-out order of shrimp with lobster sauce on the kitchen table and started stripping off her work clothes as she made her way to the bedroom. For the first time in two weeks she'd actually managed to get home before dark. She had her quiet evening at home all planned. A long leisurely bubble bath, Chinese food in bed, and a good night's sleep. She hoped Marc would phone early from Pittsburgh. Last night it had been close to midnight when he'd rung her. The poor guy was working day and night on his latest project. Hannah knew that when he did get home on Saturday he'd be bushed and it would take him at least a week or two to unwind. Chances were, she thought glumly, he'd sack out most nights in the spare room. His tune-out time, he called it. Not that she didn't have her tune-out time, too. A result of work overload. Unfortunately, the result of all the tune-out time left little time for tuning in to each other.

Hannah was down to her bra and panties, and pouring apple-scented bubble bath powder into the tub of running water when the downstairs buzzer rang. Cursing under her breath, she shut the water off, threw on a terry robe and hurried over to the intercom in the hall.

"Hi, Mrs. Welles. It's Elliot Bloomenthal. I . . . uh . . . have some papers I wanted to leave with you for your husband."

Hannah felt a rush of anxiety. "Oh . . . you can . . . just leave the papers with the doorman, Mr. Bloomenthal." She couldn't bring herself to call him Elliot. How could she be Mrs. Welles and he be Elliot? Not to mention that she wasn't really *Mrs. Welles*, since she'd kept her maiden name. For some reason she felt better having Bloomenthal think of her as *Mrs.*

"If it isn't too inconvenient for you," Bloomenthal said after a pause, "I'd like to go over a few points so that you can fill Marc in. It won't take more than ten minutes of your time."

"I was . . . just about to take a bath."

"Oh, I see. I guess I could . . . go get some coffee or something and stop back in . . . ."

"No, that's all right," she relented. "If it really won't take very long."

"Oh, it won't."

"Just give me five minutes to . . . get ready. I'll buzz."

"Fine. Thanks. I appreciate this."

Five minutes later, dressed in jeans and a shirt, Hannah opened the door for Elliot Bloomenthal. He had not only brought along papers for Marc, he presented Hannah with a dozen roses.

"Really... Mr. Bloomenthal... there's no reason..." Hannah stammered as he gave them to her.

"Elliot. And consider them a belated get-well gift." He smiled, giving Hannah a long look. "Besides, I do feel partly responsible for that accident. If I hadn't come home with your husband..."

"Oh, please, Mr....Elliot, could we just forget about that... night?"

He laughed softly. And sexily, Hannah noted with an escalating case of the jitters. "Well, Mrs. Welles, that's not so easy to do, but I'll try."

"Hannah," she relented. "Call me Hannah." It was obvious he'd intended to make a point out of the formal address until she'd given him permission to do otherwise.

"Hannah." He rolled the name on his tongue, giving it a long taste, savoring it. "Yes, it's a beautiful name. And it suits you."

Oh, God, Hannah thought, a come-on. A certifiable come-on from one of her husband's most prominent clients. But that wasn't the worst of it. The worst part was, she could feel herself responding to it. A swooping wave of guilt, shame and arousal swept over her.

"You wanted to go over some points... for Marc," she stammered.

"Hadn't you better put those roses in water first?"

"What? Oh. Yes. Right." Hannah turned abruptly and headed for the kitchen.

Elliot Bloomenthal followed.

"Nice apartment. And good security. That's important. Especially when you're alone," Elliot remarked.

"I'm not alone that much," Hannah said defensively.

"How long have you and Marc been married?"

Hannah ran tap water into a glass vase, a wedding gift from one of Marc's uncles. "Seven months."

"Ah, seven months," he echoed.

She cast him a look over her shoulder. "Why do you say it like that?"

"Seventh month. That's a tough one. Surely, you've heard of the seven-month itch?" He gave her a teasing, provocative smile, his dancing blue eyes doing a veritable tango.

"That's seven-year. Seven-*year* itch."

He grinned. "Most couples these days don't make it seven years."

Hannah shut off the water and stuck the roses haphazardly into the vase. "Well, I intend to make it seven years. I happen to believe in marriage lasting a lifetime."

While she was speaking, Elliot was lifting up her take-out carton of Chinese food. "Is this your dinner?"

"Yes."

"Oh, Hannah. This stuff is filled with unhealthy chemicals, cornstarch, soggy veggies." He carried the carton over to the trash.

"What are you doing?" she gasped as he dumped it out. "You have no right . . ."

"You need some looking after, Hannah. You need a good healthy dinner, a little fresh air, an evening of fun and relaxation."

"I . . . I don't need any such thing," she said, backing away as he walked toward her.

"You're overworked. I bet you hardly ever take time out. You miss so much, Hannah. You're missing out on some of the best parts of life."

"That's . . . not true." He was still approaching and she'd backed up to the refrigerator.

"When's the last time you went out dining in a romantic, candlelit spot, took a buggy ride around the park, went dancing under the stars . . . ?"

"No one in Manhattan takes buggy rides in the park after dark and lives to tell about it."

He stopped just an arm's length away from her. "Okay, how about the dining and dancing?" he persisted.

"Marc and I have dined . . . and danced." Hannah's heart was racing and her palms were sweaty.

"When was the last time?"

"Oh, please, Mr. Bloomenthal. A marriage is not dining and dancing. A marriage is . . . is . . ."

"Yes, Mrs. Welles?"

She gave him a weak look. "Please . . . could we just go over those papers."

"Over dinner."

"No. I . . . I can't."

"A business dinner with a client. Surely there's nothing improper in that."

"Please, Mr. Bloomenthal, you are not my client."

"Please, Elliot." He smiled widely, his perfect pearly white teeth good enough for a toothpaste commercial. "Please Elliot and let him take you to dinner."

"I . . . can't. I'm not even dressed . . . for going out." What was so distressing to Hannah was that she was tempted. Temptation. Married only seven months and already tempted. Oh, God, maybe there really was a seven-month itch. *You're okay, Hannah, as long as you don't scratch it.*

Elliot turned, and for a minute Hannah thought with relief that he was going to leave. But instead of exiting the kitchen door, he went to the wall phone.

"Who are you calling?"

He gave her a wry smile as he dialed. "If Mohammed won't come to the mountain, the mountain will have to come to Mohammed." He spoke into the phone. "Yes, I'd like to order a couple of dinners to be delivered. How's your veal scallopini tonight? Great . . ."

"No," Hannah called out, hurrying over to the phone.

"Hold on a minute," he said to the person on the line. And then to Hannah. "You don't want the veal?"

"It isn't that," she started to say, but before she could complete the sentence, Elliot said into the phone, "Two orders of veal scallopini delivered to 439 Park Avenue, apartment 12C. And a bottle of your best Chianti."

"You shouldn't have done that," Hannah said sharply after Elliot hung up. "Do you behave this way with all your clients' wives?"

He grinned. "Only the beautiful ones."

"That's disgusting."

"Hannah, I'm joking. I've never behaved this way with any other wife, client or otherwise. I guess, the truth is, I haven't been able to get you out of my mind since the first time—"

"Please," she pleaded.

"I know, I promised I'd try to forget the way you looked that night, but . . ."

"I was dressed that way for my husband."

"Hannah, can I ask you a personal question?"

"No."

"Are you and Marc happily married?"

"I said no."

"No, you're not happily married?"

"No, you can't ask me a personal question."

He smiled, his blue-eyed gaze fixed on her. "Hannah, I'm not the sort of man to pull any punches. I find you extraordinarily attractive. I know you're married, and believe me, I have all the respect in the world for the institution of marriage, but sometimes a woman has . . . special needs, a craving for excitement, liberation, a chance to experience her most secret fantasies. Think about it, Hannah. . . ."

"I am thinking, Mr. Bloomenthal," she said tightly, grabbing the roses out of the vase and shoving them in his chest, the dripping wet stems trickling drops of water down his trousers. "I am thinking that you'd better leave. As for the papers, why don't you see Marc in his office on Monday."

A minute later, Hannah slammed the front door shut behind the flabbergasted Mr. Bloomenthal then headed for the telephone.

"Hi, Pam. Did you eat dinner yet?"

"No. I was going to go down to the deli for a corn beef sandwich."

"I've got a couple of orders of veal scallopini on the way. And a bottle of Chianti."

"Great. I'll be there in a jif."

"So," PAM PRODDED, sipping her Chianti. "Are you going to tell me how come you came to order two gourmet veal scallopini dinners for yourself?"

Hannah sighed. "One was supposed to be for Elliot Bloomenthal."

"Oh."

"Is that all you can say? Oh?"

"Oh . . . tell me more," Pam said with a grin.

"He came over tonight and...and...propositioned me. I threw him out, but not before he called in those orders."

Pam smiled. "You should feel flattered, Hannah."

"I don't feel flattered. I feel guilty."

"What for? You said you threw him out. Or did something more happen between his ordering this delicious scallopini and you ordering him out the door?"

"No. No, of course not. I wouldn't cheat on Marc. I love my husband." Hannah took a long swallow of Chianti, finishing off her glass and then stared into the empty bottom. "Oh, Pam, for a minute there, I was . . . tempted. I was attracted to Elliot Bloomenthal."

Pam refilled Hannah's glass. "Of course you were attracted to him. Who wouldn't be?"

Hannah took a sip of her refill. "Maybe . . . maybe getting married wasn't the smartest thing to do. I feel like Marc and I are . . . drifting apart. No. I guess that's not really it. You can't drift apart if you've never come together. Marc and I hardly ever see each other. And when we do, we're both too wiped out to . . . do much of anything."

"Like sex?" Pam asked gently.

Hannah nodded. "Not only sex, of course. Everything we do together feels like it's being squeezed in. We speak, but we don't really talk. We have sex, but we don't really touch. We're both so stressed out. I love Marc, Pam. He's a wonderful man. And I know he loves me. We're both trying . . . so hard, but . . . but I'm miserable. And I think Marc's miserable, too, only he's too kind and sweet and wonderful to admit it."

Pam smiled affectionately at her troubled friend. "Hannah, you can't just sit around crying into your Chianti. You've got to do something about the problem."

"What do I do?" There was a note of desperation in Hannah's voice.

"Well, actually, I have just the thing. Remember a few months back, I was telling you about this fantastic book by Rusman. . . ."

"I don't think a self-help book is going to do the trick, Pam."

"That's not what I was going to suggest. Rusman doesn't only write books about marriage, he runs workshops around the country that are specifically designed to deal with stress reduction. And, talk about perfect timing, guess where his next workshop is going to be held?"

Hannah looked at Pam. "New York?"

"At the Roosevelt Hotel. In about three weeks. It's a weekend seminar so it won't interfere with work. Marc will be back home. Hannah, it's just the thing. A whole weekend to explore the tensions in your marriage, learn how to relax and enjoy yourselves more."

"I don't know," Hannah hesitated. "It seems like a pretty drastic measure."

"A drastic measure is seeing your lawyer. You attend Rusman's workshop to prevent a drastic measure."

Still, Hannah prevaricated. "What do I tell Marc? Guess what, darling. Our marriage is a flop and we have to go spend a weekend with a psychiatrist and a whole group of marital misfits."

"No. You tell Marc that the two of you have been under a lot of stress lately because you're both in such high-power jobs, and that stress is affecting your marriage and wouldn't it be great to attend a workshop that teaches you how to reduce stress."

Hannah smiled. "You make it sound so simple. Stress reduction, huh?"

"It could change your whole marriage, Hannah."

"For better or worse?"

Pam looked Hannah straight in the eye. "How much worse can it get?"

HANNAH WAS HALF ASLEEP when the phone rang.

"Hey. Did I wake you, darling?"

"Marc?"

"How many other men phone you at eleven-fifteen at night and call you darling?"

Hannah laughed softly. "None. All the others call before ten."

"How come you're not burning the midnight oil tonight?"

"I was exhausted. It was a . . . hectic day. Oh, by the way, one of your clients dropped by with some papers."

"Oh. Who?"

"Bloomenthal."

"Oh. He dropped by the apartment?"

"Yes. Well . . . anyway, I told him it might be better if he brought the papers over to your office since . . . uh . . . he wanted to make some comments . . . about the papers."

"Hannah, you sound funny."

"Funny? No. I'm just . . . tired." She paused. "Actually Marc, I feel sort of . . . stressed out."

"Stressed out?"

"Yes, don't you? I mean, the pressures mount and there are deadlines, and travel, and clients' needs, and bosses breathing down your neck, and the rush hour traffic, and no time for . . . a nice candlelit dinner, or . . . or dancing under the stars, or . . . buggy rides. . . ."

"Buggy rides?"

"Stress, Marc. I don't understand why you're being so dense," she snapped, her pitch rising. "You can't deny we're both under stress."

"Well . . . sure. I guess we are."

"There. You see."

"Hannah, listen. When I come home on Saturday, if it would make you feel . . . less stressed . . . we'll take a buggy ride. Okay?"

"A buggy ride," Hannah said slowly, "wasn't exactly what I had in mind. I have a much better idea."

"Okay, darling," Marc murmured into the phone. "You have had some delectable ideas in the past. Mmmm. I can't wait."

Now the question was, would Marc be just as inspired when he found himself in the enthusiastic grasp of the good Dr. Rusman?

10

Till Stress Do Us Part

Roosevelt Hotel

"PLEASE, MARC," Dr. Rusman cajoled in his thick Germanic accent, "you must trust your breathing. Remember, we are once again learning to breathe like babies. Babies breathe naturally, but as we grow older and stresses mount, our breathing gets restricted. Now, again, inhale a complete and natural breath."

Marc felt ridiculous, but he tried to remember all of the steps—lifting the diaphragm, attempting to somehow fill first the middle and then the upper part of his lungs.

"The shoulders, Marc. The shoulders. Raise them... No, too much."

Hannah, who was sitting yoga style on the floor next to Marc, gave him an encouraging smile. Marc did not smile back. He hadn't been too thrilled in the first place about attending this workshop on marital stress reduction, and he was growing more disgruntled by the minute. It didn't help matters any that Hannah and the other four couples in the group seemed to be having no trouble whatsoever breathing like babies.

"No, no, too fast. You are breathing too quickly, Marc," Dr. Rusman scolded. "You must not rush your breathing. Proper breathing relieves stress. Improper breathing encourages stress. Discipline. Discipline. Feel the tension. A smile. A smile when you breathe. No, Marc. That's a grimace."

Perversely, the more Rusman tried to instruct Marc in proper breathing technique, the more rapid Marc's breathing became. Hannah looked on with alarm as Marc started to turn blue from hyperventilation.

As the rest of the group went on to the next exercise, alternative breathing in which you first held one nostril closed, then the other, Marc sat hunched over, breathing into a paper bag.

HANNAH SAT CROSS-LEGGED, eyes closed, trying to do a visualization exercise in which she was to create a relaxing image, replete with sight, taste, sound and smell.

"You are having trouble, yes?" Rusman asked her.

Hannah opened her eyes and gave the eminent doctor a puzzled look. "How did you know?"

"Your body betrays you, Hannah. Listen to your breathing. Observe the tense muscles in the neck and shoulders. Your entire body is being trapped by an invisible constricting band. There, behind your eyeball. There, at the left wall of your nose, across your teeth. It moves down your body, this band, constricting, creating muscular tension. There, at your chest, at your thighs."

To Hannah's dismay, the rest of the group all opened their eyes and followed this invisible band down her whole body.

"Well . . . it's just . . . I don't really have time to relax," Hannah admitted, feeling as if she were on display. And worse, feeling this so-called invisible band. She could even feel pressure on her teeth.

"Ah, that indicates that you are not in harmony with life, with yourself, with your partner." Rusman gave her a pitying look. "In marriage, we must seek periods of mutual relaxation. Tell me, Hannah, Marc, what do you do together for relaxation?"

Hannah looked at Marc. Marc looked at Hannah. They both looked mutely at Rusman.

"Walks in the park?" one of the group members prodded.

Hannah and Marc both shook their heads.

"Dinner out?" someone else suggested.

"When we do find time to go out together to dinner, one or the other of us usually has a client along," Marc admitted.

"Sometimes we have to combine business with pleasure," Hannah pointed out.

"Ah, killing two birds with one stone," Rusman reflected.

"Why, yes," Hannah said, brightening. "Exactly."

"Examine that image, Hannah. Killing a bird with a stone. Is that, then, your vision of relaxation, fun?" Rusman inquired.

Hannah gave Marc a helpless look. "Well . . . no. Marc, help me explain what I mean."

But, instead of coming to her rescue, Marc frowned. "Really, Hannah, that isn't a very flattering image."

Hannah felt a rush of anger. Rusman observed her closely and smiled. "Now," he said mysteriously, "we begin to make progress."

"TIM AND I FIGHT all the time about his mother always interfering in our lives," Rhonda, the petite blond computer programmer in the group, complained.

"At least my mother shows an interest," her burly husband, Tim, a physical education teacher, countered. "Your mother never even sends me a birthday card."

"Jerry and I get along fine with our in-laws." This from Ellie, a large-boned woman in her mid-thirties who was a stock analyst. "It's his bachelor friends that we get into fights about."

"Before we got married, you used to think my friends were great," Jerry, a heavyset man with thick black-rimmed glasses and a receding hairline, argued. "Now that you're a hotshot on Wall Street, they're bums."

"They *are* bums."

"Our biggest arguments," confessed Janet, a plump brunette real estate agent in her early thirties, "are over money. True, Dennis does bring home the bigger paycheck, but I don't think that gives him the right to go out and buy a stereo or a fancy sports car without even consulting me."

"I work plenty hard for that money," Dennis, a slick-looking, expensively dressed insurance agent, challenged. "And I get sick and tired of your lectures telling me how I can and should spend it."

"We fight over money, too, but mostly we fight about sex," the cool, slender, beautifully outfitted Lauren confided, much to her journalist husband Mel's chagrin.

"Damn it, Lauren, you swore you weren't going to get into any personal stuff."

Lauren gave Mel a haughty look. "That's just the point, Mel. With you sex isn't personal."

"What's that supposed to mean?" he snickered. "I'm just an animal, right?"

"You said it, not me."

"Most women would be jumping for joy if their husbands wanted them all the time."

"Me, for one," Janet piped in. "Dennis would rather putter with his car or his fishing equipment than putter with . . ." She blushed. "Rather than pay any attention to me."

"Maybe if you weren't on my case all the time," Dennis challenged his wife.

"Maybe if you showed a little tenderness and affection outside the bedroom . . ."

"Maybe if you showed some inside the bedroom . . ."

"See that, Lauren," Mel said. "Poor Jane there has to go begging. When's the last time you had to ask?"

"It might be nice to ask for a change, Mel," Lauren retorted.

During all of these heated marital interchanges, Hannah and Marc remained smugly mute. Finally, Dr. Rusman looked over at them.

"You are both very silent. What do you two argue about? Sex? Money? Work?"

"We . . . don't argue." Hannah quirked a nervous smile.

"No, we don't," Marc agreed. "Fighting is definitely not a source of stress in our relationship," he added proudly.

The other couples gave them a mix of looks—envy, disbelief, even pity. After a good rousing fight, there was always the making-up time. As for Dr. Rusman, he wore one of his enigmatic smiles.

"It is often the case," the doctor said, after a long pause, "that repressed anger causes even greater stress than anger poorly expressed."

"That's assuming it's repressed," Marc countered.

"Anger is so unconstructive," Hannah said, clearing her throat. "It's not that I repress anger really—" She stopped, smiling weakly at Marc. "We seem to spend so little time together, I don't want to use any of it up fighting."

"I didn't know there was something to fight about," Marc said warily.

"Well, I didn't say there was," Hannah replied defensively.

Dr. Rusman smiled benignly. "But if you were to have something to fight about, what would it be, Hannah?"

Hannah flushed, feeling she had been put on the spot. "Well...I suppose...I do get frustrated sometimes that Marc isn't sensitive to some of my...needs."

"Like what?" Marc asked.

Hannah nervously pushed her hair away from her face. "Well...I sometimes get the feeling that you hardly even...notice me. You never tell me that I...look nice, or...you like my dress—"

"See Dennis," Janet broke in. "I'm not the only one who complains that her husband never pays any compliments. But, see some fancy sports car pass us by, and you're practically drooling."

"Please, Hannah, go on," Rusman prodded, cutting Dennis off before he got to retort. "You feel Marc takes you for granted."

"That isn't true," Marc protested.

Rusman placed a hand on his shoulder. "You will have your turn, Marc. Go on, Hannah. What else bothers you?"

Hannah swallowed. If this exercise was supposed to be reducing stress, it wasn't working. Hannah felt like a tightly sprung wire. She looked down at the floor. "Well . . . sometimes . . . I get the feeling . . . that Marc's sort of . . . like Dennis. I mean . . . he certainly isn't lusting after me all the time. Hardly . . . any of the time."

"I lust," Marc protested. "I lusted plenty when you were out in Denver."

"And I lusted when you were out in Pittsburgh," Hannah shot back. "Not to mention all the nights you go off to sleep in the spare room—"

"So I won't disturb you while you're working till all hours of the night. Sometimes, Hannah, I think you work all night so that you can avoid—"

"I do not avoid—"

"What about that day in our new apartment? You had me half-undressed. I want you. I want you, you said. And then your damn office calls and—"

"It was very important."

Marc threw up his hands in disgust. "Right. More important than me."

"Isn't this a case of the pot calling the kettle black?" Hannah could feel her pulse racing. She glared at Marc. "You always put your work ahead of me. CSR eats up all your time and energy. My mother was right. We don't have fun, excitement, passion. I have needs, Marc. . . ."

"Do you, Hannah? I can't see them. You're so damn self-sufficient, self-reliant, independent. I sometimes wonder why it was you married me in the first place."

Hannah stared at Marc, shocked and hurt. "Why...because...I loved you. And because...I thought we were so well matched. But now—" She stopped, close to tears, aware of the silent stares of the other members of the group.

"But now...?" Rusman coaxed.

Hannah shook her head.

"No, go on, Hannah. Spill it out. Let's get it all out on the table," Marc said angrily. "This was your idea. Hey, we're supposed to let our hair down, tell it like it is. You don't want to repress your anger, Hannah. Think of all that stress. Go on. Take one of Dr. Rusman's deep, natural breaths and say what you have to say."

"I never knew you could be...sarcastic."

"Maybe there are a lot of things about me you don't know," Marc retorted.

"Like what?" she demanded.

"Like what? I'll tell you like what? Like I'm...jealous, that's what. Like I don't like the idea of you getting chummy with my clients."

"What clients?"

"Bloomenthal, for one."

Hannah's mouth dropped open. "I...Bloomenthal...chummy?"

"Oh, Hannah, I saw that get-well florist card, signed Elliot. What'd you do, toss the flowers he obviously brought you, before I got back home from Pittsburgh?"

"You never said a word."

"Okay, well, I'm saying it now."

"You're saying you don't trust me."

"And I suppose you trust me? That's why you barged into my apartment when Robin was there?"

"She was there, all right. Wrapped in your arms."

"I explained all that."

"Right. And as for Bloomenthal, there's nothing to explain," Hannah snapped.

Rusman rubbed his hands together in glee. "Yes, yes, now we are confronting what I call the hidden stress chafers. Ah, how they irritate, how they fester. How they chafe! Untie them my friends. Shout out—I am jealous. I am insecure. I am not sure of your love. I don't know who you are. I don't know what I am doing in this relationship." The doctor leapt from his chair. "This is the beginning. Whenever these chafing emotions take hold, you must acknowledge them. Shout," he commanded. "Don't be embarrassed."

But Marc didn't shout. Instead, he just stared at Hannah in stony silence as if he were seeing a stranger.

Hannah sprang up, a desperate look on her face. "I've got to . . . leave. I've got . . . a terrible headache."

As she started for the door, Rusman shouted after her, "No, no. This is your inner stress speaking, Hannah. A flight response. You must use mastery. Remember your breathing, Hannah. Visualization . . . The constricting band . . . Notice the sensations . . ."

As Marc started after Hannah, Rusman tried to block his progress. Marc glared at him. "Get out of my way, doc, or you'll be noticing some sensations."

452 Grammercy Park

"OF COURSE I'M HAPPY for you, Mother." Hannah plastered a smile on her face as she sat in her mother's living room. "It's . . . wonderful. It's just . . . that it seems so sudden. I mean . . . you've only known Simon for a few months. Marriage is such a . . . big step." Hannah's smile faded.

"I agree," Mary Logan said, her smile luminescent. "And I don't want you to think this is a frivolous decision, Hannah. Simon and I may not have known each other that long, but we've spent so much time together and we've been very open and honest with each other."

"Have you?" Hannah murmured.

Mary Logan smiled. "Simon knows I have my . . . quirks. I told him I can be pushy and demanding. And while I try to hide it, I've admitted to him that I'm impossibly sentimental. And I'm used to having my own way."

"And Simon's been equally frank?"

Mary Logan smiled slyly. "Men always seem to find it harder to open up and reveal their vulnerabilities. Simon isn't an exception, but I've tried very hard to assure him that I'm not looking for the perfect man. And little by little he has shared some of his fears and concerns. Like he's quite terrified of growing old. He can be vain, but deep down he's just scared he won't be loved for who he is inside."

Mary's face glowed. Hannah thought her mother looked ten years younger. And so happy.

Mary took hold of her daughter's hand. "The other night Simon confessed that he's always been a little bit afraid of the dark. When he's alone he always leaves a light on in the hall and keeps his bedroom door ajar. I was . . . so touched. I feel that we can tell each other anything. We're good together, Hannah. We truly enjoy each other's company, we like doing the same things, we have such good times together. I haven't laughed so much in years. Did I tell you Simon has a boat. You know how I used to love to sail. Your father hated boats. He hated the water. We always had to take our vacations in the mountains. Simon and I are going to spend our honeymoon sailing around the Canary Islands."

"That's . . . nice."

"You might sound a bit more enthusiastic. What is it, Hannah? Don't you like Simon?"

Hannah rose from her mother's couch and meandered over to the fireplace. On the mantel was one of the photos Marc's brother-in-law had taken of her and Marc fitted out in borrowed bridal gown and tux. The *wedding* photo, Hannah thought, was a mockery. Everything about her marriage was a mockery. Tears started to trickle down her cheeks. She didn't hear her mother approach.

"You look so drawn, Hannah. And so unhappy," Mary Logan said softly, putting an arm around her daughter. "Talk to me, Hannah."

"I envy you, Mother. I envy you and Simon. It must be nice to have all the time in the world to be with each other. No other responsibilities, no stress . . ."

"Hannah, don't idealize our relationship. Of course Simon and I have responsibilities and stresses. Even though Simon's officially retired, he's still involved with his company. And I have my volunteer work, my friends. We've both been divorced for years and have our separate interests and involvements. Then there are the typical health issues that come with our ages. And there's Simon's son who is taking a rather critical view of his father's remarriage. There are stresses, Hannah. But there are also joys. And I need joy. So does Simon. Neither of us wants to grow old alone and joyless."

"Neither...neither do I," Hannah said, tears streaming down her face.

Mary put her arms around her daughter. "Oh, Hannah."

"What am I going to do, Mother? I'm so...miserable. And Marc's so miserable. We've tried. A few weeks ago we even went to a ... a workshop."

"What kind of a workshop?" Mary asked, guiding her daughter back to the couch.

"Oh, it was so dumb. We did these stupid exercises and then the other couples started talking about all their petty arguments, and ... and Marc and I were feeling so...superior because we...we never bicker. And then we did. Right in front of all these strangers, Marc ... attacked me."

"Attacked you?" Mary said with alarm.

"Verbally attacked me, which is ... something I ... I never thought Marc would ... do. And he was sarcastic and ... rude ... and he told me ... he told me ..." Hannah pressed her face against her mother's chest.

Mary patted Hannah's hair. "What did he tell you, darling?"

"He . . . he told me I was . . . self-sufficient . . . self-reliant . . . independent. He . . . he told me . . . he didn't even think I had any . . . needs."

"Well, of course you do," Mary soothed, rubbing her daughter's back.

"Of course . . . I do. So why is he so . . . so dense?"

"Men can be dense, Hannah."

CSR

MARC CRUMPLED UP the paper he'd been working on and tossed it in the trash, missing it by a mile. John Moss, who was working at the desk across the way looked over at Marc and gave him a sympathetic smile. "Problems?"

"I don't know what's wrong with me," Marc muttered. "I can't seem to concentrate lately."

"I . . . uh . . . guess that Rusman workshop you and Hannah went to didn't do the trick."

Marc gave Moss a sharp look. "How did you know about the workshop?"

John Moss smiled sheepishly. "Pam mentioned it to me. We've gone out a few times. Nothing serious or anything. She's a sharp cookie, though." John ambled over to Marc's desk. "Pam was real surprised that you and Hannah didn't find the workshop helpful. I don't know. Pam even said she thought that if Liz and I'd gone to something like that, you know, dealt with our stress more effectively, maybe we'd have made our marriage work." He shrugged. "I didn't want to bust Pam's balloon, but I don't really think these marriage experts have the answers."

"I wonder," Marc mused, "what Rusman's marriage is like. You think he and his wife have it made?"

John chuckled. "Are you kidding? Nine will get you ten, he's divorced. Most of these so-called experts are, you know. They can't figure the game out any more than we can."

Marc stared glumly down at the open file on his desk. "I thought I understood Hannah. Now, I can't figure her out at all. I don't know what she wants."

"Take it from me, neither does she," John assured him. "Your best bet is not to try to figure her out. Women hate to be figured out, Welles. Believe me, I know. The minute I figured my wife out, she sued for divorce."

439 Park Avenue

"HI." MARC loosened his tie as he walked into the apartment. "I didn't think you'd be home yet."

Hannah smiled as she observed her husband. "You look naked."

Marc glanced down at his blue suit, then gave Hannah a puzzled look.

"No briefcase."

He laughed. "I left it at the office." He walked over and kissed Hannah lightly on the cheek. "What are you doing home so early?"

"I . . . uh . . . took the afternoon off."

Marc looked surprised. "Aren't you feeling okay?"

"I spent the afternoon with my mother." She paused. "Discussing her trousseau."

"What?"

"She and Simon are getting married."

"Your mother's getting married?"

"Don't sound so astonished."

"They haven't known each other that long."

"Time's relative. It's what you do with it."

Marc observed Hannah warily. "We aren't going to argue, are we, Hannah?"

"No," she said in a low voice. "Let's not argue."

Marc touched her cheek. "You look very pretty tonight." He rested his hands on her shoulders. "I guess I don't tell you that enough."

She let her head drop to his shoulder and sank against him. "Oh, Marc, this isn't how I pictured wedded bliss. We should never have gone to that dumb workshop. Maybe we did have stress before, but at least I didn't know it was so complicated. Now we know and...and it's worse."

"Yeah, but think about those other couples at the workshop," Marc reflected. "I don't know. As marriages go, maybe we aren't so bad off."

Hannah smiled wryly. "That isn't exactly saying a hell of a lot."

"It will get . . . better."

She gave him a sharp look. "You hesitated."

"What? When?"

"You don't really think it will get better. You're sorry we got married, aren't you? You think we were better off . . . before we said I do."

"When did I say that? You're putting words into my mouth, Hannah."

"I'm just saying your own thoughts out loud."

"How can you speak my thoughts? If anyone is going to speak my thoughts it should be me."

"You don't speak, Marc. You . . . you . . . imply."

"Imply? What do I imply?"

"You imply that you're sorry we got married."

"I am not sorry, Hannah," Marc said emphatically.

"Then why are you shouting?"

"To prove to you I do speak, not imply."

"Okay, then tell me you're happy. Tell me you're a happily married man and that you don't have any regrets."

Marc took in a deep breath. "Hannah, I thought we weren't going to argue."

"I'm not arguing. Just answer one simple question. And I want you to be absolutely honest with me, Marc. I promise I won't cry or get angry, or . . . anything." She stared him straight in the eye. "If you had it to do over again . . . marrying me, I mean . . . would you do it?"

"That question is pointless, Hannah. We are married. And I want to stay married. Isn't that the point?" He went to reach for her, but she darted away.

"That's one point, but it's a different point. Yes, we are married. And neither of us likes failure. Neither of us is a quitter. We like to be good at everything we do. We keep plugging. But . . . if we weren't married . . . if we turned the clocks back nine months . . . and we had it to do all over again, would you marry me?"

Marc adjusted the gold band of his Rolex, then returned his gaze to hers. "Knowing everything we know?"

Hannah felt an invisible clamp tighten around her. Dr. Rusman's damn constricting band. Slowly, she nodded. "Yes, knowing everything we know."

He didn't answer for what felt to Hannah like an eternity. "No," he said finally, emitting a long sigh first. "I guess if I were to be absolutely truthful, and you did say you wanted me to be absolutely truthful, I'd have to say no, I probably wouldn't have gotten married. In general. I mean . . . marriage is so much more complicated than I thought at the time. If I'd known all the complications, I think I'd have decided to stay a bachelor. But," he quickly added, seeing Hannah's color pale, "if I didn't know . . . everything I know . . . I'd do it again, Hannah. I'd marry you all over again. And, more important, knowing everything I know, I wouldn't not want to be married to you right now. Does that make sense?"

"No," she said tightly.

"Sure it does," Marc insisted. "Come on, Hannah. The point is, we've lived through the complications. And we've also had some glorious moments. It's like a roller coaster. Maybe if you knew how wild a ride it was going to be you would have passed. But, say you don't know, and you get on. And once you're on the roller coaster, once you're experiencing the thrill, the craziness, even the terror of it, you wouldn't get off for anything. Now do you understand?"

Hannah let herself be drawn against Marc. "There's one big difference," she murmured.

Marc nibbled at her neck. "What's that, darling?"

"I don't know one person who's ever leapt off a moving roller coaster ride, but I sure as hell know plenty of people who've leapt out of a roller coaster marriage."

11

I Do. Do I?

City Hall

"EXCUSE ME, MR. HARRELL. I'm sorry to bother you, but we seem to have a problem."

"That's nothing new, Mrs. Sheldon. What is it this time?"

"It's about those marriage records we've been switching over to the new computer system."

"Yes?"

"Well, it appears that, in the changeover, we've somehow lost a day."

"Lost a day?"

"Yes, sir. The official recording of the civil marriages performed here on December twelfth of this past year seem to have...been obliterated. A...uh... glitch...in the new equipment."

"This is all I need, Mrs. Sheldon. Are you telling me that all the marriages performed on that particular day are no longer valid?"

"Well, at the moment, sir. But, it really shouldn't be too big a problem to mend. Our register indicates that there were only four marriages scheduled for that day. And, actually, all we need to do is contact the couples and have them send us a photocopy of their marriage certificates and rerecord them in the new system to re-validate them."

"Well then, that shouldn't be any problem."

"No, sir."

"Then, really, Mrs. Sheldon, there was no need for you to add to my worries, was there?"

"No, sir."

"In that case, I assume, Mrs. Sheldon, that I can trust you to see to it that this matter is tidied up quickly."

"Yes, sir."

"By Friday at the very latest, Mrs. Sheldon."

"Yes, sir. I'll get in touch with the four couples today and that will give them two days to get their marriage certificates into the office. I . . . uh . . . just hope none of the couples is out of town."

"Let's not create new problems for ourselves, Mrs. Sheldon, until they prove to be problems."

"Yes, sir."

"Oh, and Mrs. Sheldon, I see no need for this little matter to go beyond this office."

"No, sir. I mean, yes, sir. That is, I'll take care of the matter immediately.

CSR

"THERE'S A PHONE CALL for you, Mr. Welles. From a Mrs. Sheldon at City Hall. She says it's important."

Marc frowned. He was already running late for a meeting over at the other end of town. "Can you please take a message, Carrie. It's probably about those Gedron papers that were filed with the tax rebate office." He gathered up his papers. "Oh, and Carrie, I'm

going to head straight home from the Markham offices. You can tell the woman from City Hall if she needs
to speak to me in person, she can reach me on Friday,
when I get back from Detroit."

"No problem."

Unicom

"MAY I PLEASE SPEAK to Mrs. Hannah Welles. This is
Mrs. Sheldon."

"Who did you want to speak with?"

"Mrs. Welles. Hannah Welles."

"Welles? Just a minute, please."

Mrs. Sheldon pursed her lips. The Welles couple was
the last on her list. The other three couples were all very
cooperative and had agreed to either bring their marriage certificates down to the registry or mail it in via
courier service. Now, all she needed was the Welleses'
marriage certificate, and the problem would be rectified.

"No, I'm sorry. We don't have anyone by the name
of Welles listed in the Unicom directory."

"Oh, dear. Now let me see . . . How about a Hannah
Logan? Perhaps she's still using her maiden name."

"Logan. Yes. Hannah Logan. That's extension 421.
Would you like me to connect you?"

"Yes, please."

A moment later, a woman with a Brooklyn accent
got on the line. "Team Development. Ms. Russell
speaking."

"Yes, this is Mrs. Sheldon from the registry office at City Hall in Manhattan. May I please speak to Miss Logan? Hannah Logan."

"Sorry, you missed her by about twenty minutes. She's due back on Friday."

"Friday? You mean she won't be at work tomorrow or Thursday?"

"She'll be out of town on business. Would you like to leave a message?"

"Oh, dear. No. Friday's too late. Well, I suppose I'll have to try to reach her at home."

City Hall

"Operator, I've been trying a number and I can't get through. Could you please check it?" She gave the operator the number.

"One moment, please."

Mrs. Sheldon checked her watch. Six forty-five. She should have been home an hour ago. Charlie and the kids would be having a bird about having to get the dinner on the table by themselves. But what was she supposed to do? She had promised Harrell this matter would be tidily resolved by Friday. Well, at least the Welles couple was in town. Now, if she could just get one of them on the phone . . .

"I'm sorry. That number has been changed. The new number is unlisted."

"But . . . it can't be. This is official city business. Surely—"

"I'm sorry. We cannot give out any unlisted numbers."

"But, I'm trying to tell you, this is—"

"Would you like to speak to my supervisor?"

"Yes... Oh, no. Never mind," Mrs. Sheldon snapped, hanging up the phone. A moment later she was re-dialing Marc Welles's business number on the off chance his secretary was working overtime and would give her his home number.

Receiving no answer at CSR, she tried Unicom. No luck there, either. Finally, she dialed the motor vehicle bureau and got Marc's current address. Then she dialed her own home number. Her husband, Charlie, was none too happy about hearing her news.

"Yes, well I'm sorry, Charlie. I know you feel it's im-portant for us to all have dinner together. I feel the same way. But this can't be helped. I've got to get a hold of this couple tonight. I know for certain both the wife and the husband are going to be out of town until Friday, which means I won't have this mess fixed on time and Harrell will have my head. And, since their home number is unlisted, I'll just have to go over to their apartment and explain the problem in person. Ac-tually, it's just as well if they have their marriage cer-tificate on hand. Then I can just take it along with me and this whole awkward problem will be rectified."

"You mean," Charlie asked with a chuckle, "that un-til you record those certificates these couples aren't of-ficially married?"

"No, not really. As long as they have their signed certificates, their marriages are basically valid. But, of course, if any of the couples were to misplace their cer-tificate or if there were a fire or something and the cer-tificate were destroyed, and they requested a new one from City Hall, we wouldn't be able to reissue one unless we had the marriage recorded on our computers."

"So, you better cross your fingers this last couple's got their certificate."

Bea Sheldon smiled. "Oh, I'm sure they do. Not even married a year yet. They've probably still got it tied in red ribbon in a special keepsake box. Or in their vault, which will simply mean the husband will have to get it in the morning and send it over to us by courier."

Charlie Sheldon chuckled again. "Hey Bea, you know what this means, don't ya? If any of those poor henpecked hubbies want out, all they have to do is burn their certificates and—poof—they're bachelors again."

Bea Sheldon pursed her lips. "What about the poor put-upon wives, Charlie, whose husbands are always coming home late, tracking in dirt, leaving their clothes all over the house, complaining about how their wives don't have supper on the table, or they look dragged out, or—"

"Hey, hey, what are ya saying, doll? If you were one of them couples, you'd rip up your marriage certificate and be single again?"

Bea Sheldon smiled. "Oh, Charlie, are you kidding? Not on your life."

"Yeah, that's my girl."

"What about you, Charlie? You wish you could go back to being a bachelor again?"

Charlie chuckled. "No way, doll. I never had it so good." His chuckle deepened. "Even if I do cluck-cluck every now and then."

"Oh, Charlie. I love you."

"Listen here, Bea. You take a cab over to this place. And then you take a cab on home. No subways after dark. I don't care about the cost. Or maybe ya want me to meet ya over at this apartment and we'll go home together. I can get Jeannie next door to sit for the kids."

"Maybe we can even stop on the way home and have a drink."

"Yeah, how about Victor's Place? They've got that great little jazz combo...."

"And candlelight..."

"Ya look like an angel in candlelight, doll...."

439 Park Avenue

"YOU'RE NOT STILL MAD at me about the other night, are you, Hannah?"

Hannah was tearing lettuce into a salad bowl while Marc was putting a couple of steaks on a broiler pan. "Mad about what?"

"You know about what?" Marc said, his voice measured. "About that dumb question."

"Dumb?" Hannah started ripping the lettuce leaf into shreds. "There was nothing dumb about it. I merely asked if you had it to do all over again, would you marry me."

"So, you do remember," Marc said with a faint smile.

"I also remember your answer," she said, attacking the next lettuce leaf.

Marc walked over to her and tried to turn her toward him, but she turned to stone. "Hannah, we're both trying harder now. Look, here we are, at seven-thirty, both home, preparing dinner together, sharing what

I'm sure our dear old pal, Dr. Rusman, would call chafe-reduction time. Why even think about what we might or might not have done in the past? We have the present and the future to think about, Hannah. Hey, do you know we're only a month away from our first wedding anniversary? One whole year, Hannah. Mr. and Mrs. for one whole year. Even if you don't use the Mrs." He kissed the tip of her nose. "What would you like to do to celebrate our first anniversary?"

Hannah gave him a weary smile. "You've got to be in L.A. on business on our anniversary, remember. And my London trip for Unicom is still a strong possibility." What she hadn't yet told Marc was that Unicom was seriously considering going international and a London base was first on their list of locations. Hannah knew that if the trip was approved, it would mean that Briskin was moving his plan off the drawing board. There was a very good chance that, if London proved viable, she'd be the one he'd ask to start up the office. That could mean anywhere from two to six months. Even longer, if she wanted. If she wanted . . . Lately, Hannah wasn't the least bit sure what she wanted.

"Hey, I have an idea," Marc said. "If you don't go to London, how about flying out to L.A. and we'll celebrate our anniversary together in the same place?" He grinned. "It'll be a novelty."

Before Hannah could answer, the downstairs buzzer rang.

"I'll see who it is," she said. "You pop the steaks into the oven. We've got to eat, pack for our trips and try to get a decent night's sleep."

"SO YOU SEE," Mrs. Sheldon said, sitting perched on the edge of Hannah and Marc's living-room sofa, "it's really a minor matter of . . . bookkeeping. All I really need is your marriage certificate and I'll rectify our official records and everything will be in perfect order."

"Our marriage certificate," Hannah echoed, glancing over at Marc. "You took it that day at City Hall, didn't you?"

Marc made a face. "No, I don't think so, Hannah. I seem to remember you popped the certificate into your purse. No . . . no, your briefcase. Yes, I'm almost positive."

"No, Marc. I didn't take it. I remember I was running late and I was worried about catching a cab. . . ."

"Yes, and I had to get all the way over to New Jersey that afternoon. . . ."

"I'm pretty sure you stuck it in your jacket pocket, Marc. I can picture it. . . ."

Marc frowned. "One of us must have taken it. That was such a rushed day. Now, let me think for a minute. . . ."

Mrs. Sheldon looked with anxious surprise from Hannah to Marc. The other three couples had had no trouble at all in getting their hands on their marriage certificates, much less even remembering if they actually had them. She, herself, had lovingly placed her marriage certificate in an antique gold frame that hung on their bedroom wall, right beside their eight-by-ten color, glossy wedding picture.

Hannah left the room to check to see if it was either in her file cabinet or Marc's. Meanwhile, Marc offered Bea Sheldon a drink.

"No, thank you," Mrs. Sheldon said. Then, after an awkward silence she asked, "Excuse me, Mr. Welles, but do you smell something burning?"

Marc sniffed. "Oh damn. The steaks. I forgot all about the steaks." He rushed off to the kitchen to see smoke billowing out of the oven door.

Hannah returned to the living room. "We don't have it," she announced.

"Oh, dear," Mrs. Sheldon said, springing up from the couch. "You must have it."

Hannah looked for Marc. "Where did my husband go?" *Husband.* Was he officially her husband if there was no marriage certificate and no recording of the marriage in City Hall's records?

"The steaks were burning," Mrs. Sheldon explained.

Hannah sighed. "Our first dinner at home together in weeks. It figures."

"Mrs. Welles . . . you must have the marriage certificate someplace. Maybe in your vault at the bank."

Marc returned to the living room. "The steaks . . ."

"I know," Hannah said. "The steaks are burnt and our marriage certificate is nowhere to be found."

Marc frowned, shifting his gaze to Mrs. Sheldon. "What happens now?"

"Yes, what does happen now?" Hannah asked Mrs. Sheldon as well.

Mrs. Sheldon sat back down on the sofa. "Oh, dear." This was not a problem she was prepared for. Personally, she didn't agree with her boss's edict not to worry about problems before they prove to be problems.

Then, the problems just caught you unawares and it was difficult to think about how to resolve them.

Hannah and Marc looked at each other. They, too, sat down.

"I do wish you could locate the marriage certificate," Mrs. Sheldon muttered. "Really, it would be so much simpler."

"Maybe neither of us picked up the paper and it's still sitting in the registrar's desk at City Hall," Marc suggested.

"Oh, no, it isn't there. If it hadn't been picked up at the time, it would have been mailed to you within three working days." Mrs. Sheldon wore a hopeful smile. "Maybe that's what happened. Maybe you received it in the mail and tucked it away."

Hannah and Marc both pondered the possibility.

"I have no recollection," Marc said. "How about you, Hannah?"

Hannah shook her head.

Mrs. Sheldon sighed.

"I'll go check the files," Marc said, rising.

Hannah rose, too. "I'll check the desks and wherever else I can think of," she said. "We won't keep you, Mrs. Sheldon. If we track it down, we'll get it right over to City Hall."

Mrs. Sheldon regarded Hannah and Marc anxiously. "You do realize the importance of locating that certificate?"

Marc smiled. "We both work for bureaucracies, Mrs. Sheldon. We know how they like everything to be in order."

"Oh, dear, it's more important than that. You must understand . . . without the certificate . . . and with no official record of the marriage ceremony having taken place . . . why, legally, the two of you aren't . . . married." Mrs. Sheldon nervously kneaded the purse in her hands. "Of course, all you would need to do is . . . get married again. . . ."

Baited Hook Café at 57th

"WHAT DOES SHE MEAN, she isn't married?" Laura gasped, arriving late at the table, and relieved to find a chef's salad waiting at her place, thanks to Diane. She poured out the whole pitcher of Thousand Island dressing over the greens.

"She can't find her marriage certificate," Pam explained, after swallowing a bit of her roast beef sandwich.

Laura shrugged, plucking the Swiss cheese from her salad. Had she been on time to order, she would have told the waitress to switch the Swiss for cheddar. "Why, that doesn't mean anything. All you have to do, Hannah, is write for another one at City Hall."

"No can do," Diane said, putting the lettuce and tomato on her hamburger. "A computer glitch. The official record was erased. Without the marriage certificate there's no legal proof Hannah and Marc were married."

"That's crazy," Laura exclaimed.

"No," Hannah said dryly. "That's fact. Marc and I aren't married."

"Okay, so you run down to City Hall and get married again," Pam said, stabbing a French fry.

"Right," Diane said. "No big deal."

Laura brightened. "Let's throw Hannah a real wedding shower this time. We were all too busy to get one organized last December. Won't that be fun?"

"Great idea," Pam agreed. "And I was thinking, Hannah... well, I know it's none of my business, but...maybe this time, given that you have the chance to plan a second wedding, why not make a real event of it? I was reading this book by Bumbaca and Loewen called *How to Survive a Marriage*, and they make a point of saying that how you start off your marriage is a key factor in setting the tone for your future together."

Hannah gave her friend a long, bemused look. "Tell me something, Pam. Why do you read all these books on marriage when you're single?"

Pam flushed. "Why, I...I'm not single by choice, Hannah. And I feel that if I do find the right man, well, I want to know he is the right man. According to a lot of experts, most women are so busy losing their hearts over the wrong man that they let the right one go...right on by. Anyway, if I find him...and if we do get married...I want to be an informed participant. Is there anything wrong with that?"

"I think it's instinct, myself," Laura mused. A smile curved her peach-tinted lips. "No expert can teach you instinct, Pam." She turned to Hannah. "But I do think Pam has a point about having a real wedding this time."

"She had a real wedding last time," Diane countered. "It's saying the I do's that count, not where you say them. I personally don't see the point in making a big fuss over the wedding. Pretty soon you start agonizing over the gown not being right, there are fights over the guest list, some cousin is offended because she wasn't asked to be a bridesmaid, the organist is tipsy..."

"Oh, God." Laura giggled. "At our wedding, the flower girl, Don's five-year-old niece, was so nervous about walking down the aisle, she actually threw up halfway to the altar. Luckily she missed my gown."

"I was at this fabulous wedding on Long Island last month," Pam interrupted. "Ultra-chic. Corey, that was the bride, wore this absolutely-to-die-for white silk taffeta bustier dress by Beene. I heard it cost over three thousand bucks."

"And, no doubt, worth every penny," Laura said with a grin.

"If I had a few thousand bucks to throw around," Diane said, rolling her eyes, "I wouldn't waste it on a one-shot wedding gown...."

"Who says it has to be one shot?" Laura said, popping a black olive into her mouth. "She can always wear it when she marries a second time."

"Hey, just think, Hannah," Pam said, "if you'd blown big bucks on a wedding dress the first time round, you'd have been able to get a second wearing out of it."

"There isn't going to be a second wearing. I mean...a second wedding," Hannah murmured.

"Hannah's right," Pam pointed out. "In a sense, this is going to be her first wedding."

"True," Laura agreed. "It is sort of a first wedding—officially."

"Not really," Diane mused. "The first wedding was official, until the computer erased the file. So, in point of fact, this is a second wedding."

"There isn't going to be a second wedding...or a first wedding," Hannah said, moving her teriyaki chicken around her plate with her fork.

All eyes turned to her.

"What are you talking about, Hannah?" Pam said sharply.

Laura gasped. "Don't tell me Marc doesn't want to get married again."

"No," Hannah said quietly. "He says he wants to get married again. The point is, he wouldn't have gotten married the first time if he'd had it to do again."

"You're losing me," Diane said.

The others were equally lost.

Hannah had been so proud of herself up to now. She'd been cool, calm and collected. It all made perfect sense to her. Now, with three pairs of probing eyes on her, she felt a sudden loss of control. Tears threatened. Confusion swirled around in her head. "I . . . I can't explain it. It's just . . . I don't think Marc really wants to be married. And . . . maybe I don't really want to be married either. There were . . . so many factors neither Marc or I took into consideration the first time around. We had this . . . dumb limited partnership plan . . . and we thought it was going to be so simple. We kept bending over backward to be accepting and supportive and understanding. Meanwhile, we were both getting unbearable backaches. And then we started arguing, which we swore we wouldn't do . . . and we both said things we shouldn't have said.... So then we started walking on eggshells around each other."

Hannah sighed wearily. "I mean, I'd have to be crazy to go through it all again."

Pam opened her mouth to say something, but Hannah cut her off at the quick. "And don't tell me about any more brilliant ideas you read about in any of your self-help books."

Pam looked hurt. "I wasn't, Hannah. I was just going to ask you . . . Do you still love him?"

The tears Hannah'd been managing to hold back, broke through the floodgates and began dropping onto her teriyaki. "That's the worst part. I love him like crazy. But . . . I can't marry him a second time, or a first time, or . . . or any time. He doesn't want to be married. I know he doesn't."

"But he says he does," Pam said.

"What's he supposed to say?" Hannah argued. "Gee Hannah, what a lucky break. I thought I was stuck in this marriage for life because I'm not the kind of guy to renege on a contract. But hey, now that there's no contract, we can cut our losses without losing face." Hannah looked around at her friends. "Would Marc ever say that?"

They all had to admit he wouldn't. Whatever his faults, he was a decent guy. A decent guy who would always do the decent thing.

"But what if you're wrong, Hannah?" Pam persisted. "What if he's really sincere about his proposal?"

"If he was sincere about his proposal," Hannah challenged, "what's he doing packing for a business trip to L.A.?"

"What about you?" Diane asked. "I heard this morning that the London trip is on. Are you going?"

Hannah swiped at her wet cheeks with her paper napkin. "I told Briskin I'd give him my answer in three days. I told him if I did go, it would have to wait until after my mother's wedding in two weeks. He said no problem."

"Hannah, what does your mother say about you and Marc not remarrying?" Laura asked.

"She doesn't even know we're not married, yet. I haven't had the heart to tell her. She's floating on cloud nine right now. She and Simon are completely absorbed in their wedding plans and their honeymoon trip. I figure it can wait until after they get back from the Canary Islands." She blew her nose. "Besides, my mother wants me to be her matron of honor. I just can't tell her I'm not a . . . matron." Fresh tears erupted and all three women hurriedly volunteered their napkins.

10 Drowning, a bar on East 23rd

"YOU SURE YOU WANT another refill?" John Moss asked Marc. "You're not a drinker. And those manhattans can really be killers."

"Sure, he wants a refill," Harris piped in. "The guy's off the hook. This is his bachelor party. We're celebrating."

"Make it a double," Marc said, the words coming out slurry.

"I don't understand," John said, sipping his martini. "Why doesn't Hannah want to marry you again? I mean, you two never talked about getting a divorce, right?"

"Right," Marc said, blinking to get John in better focus. "No divorce. There's never been a divorce in my family. And Hannah always said…" He squinted. What was it she always said? It was right on the tip of his tongue. Problem was, his tongue was feeling a little numb. Actually his whole face felt numb. He chuckled. "I could have saved myself three hundred bucks and a weekend of sheer hell if I'd known that a few manhattans could do a lot more for stress than natural breathing, visualization, assertiveness training."

"Yeah, but you don't wake up with a hangover the morning after a workshop," John pointed out.

Marc was already feeling a little headachy and it wasn't even the next morning yet. Why, he wondered, if he was so drunk as to be a good two-thirds numb, was he still feeling so miserable?

Harris gave him a good-buddy slap on the back. "Hey man, you're better off. Think of this as a lucky break. No papers to file, no messy divorce, no alimony hassles, a nice, clean break. Face it pal, marriage wasn't exactly heaven."

"I don't know," John mused. "I really thought Marc and Hannah had a chance. Sure, the first year is always rough—"

"The firsht eleven months," Marc corrected drunkenly.

"I remember how rough the first year was for me and Liz—" John continued.

"And the second. And the third," Harris bantered.

"Yeah," John admitted. "I guess that's true. It didn't really get easier for us. But it's supposed to."

"I still say Marc's better off," Harris declared.

Marc downed half of his double manhattan. "Yeah, I'm better off. I'm glad she didn't shay yesh. I asked, right? I asked. She shaid no." He downed the rest of the manhattan and then stared forlornly into the empty glass.

John gave Marc's shoulder a supportive squeeze. "You really love her, don't you?"

Marc had a momentary flash of soberness. "More than I realized. When she shaid no . . . I felt like . . . like my whole world was coming unglued. I love her, Moss. She's . . . my glue, my . . . raison d'être, my heart, my—"

"Ball and chain," Harris muttered, grinning.

John shot Harris a sharp look, then turned back to Marc. "You could always ask her again. Maybe . . . maybe do it on your knees this time. You know what I mean. Get real romantic. Women are suckers for romance, Marc."

Slowly, Marc lifted his head. It wasn't easy. His head felt like a dead weight. Bleary-eyed, he looked hopefully at John. Both of him. "You really shink sho?"

Harris Porter smiled slyly. "Big mistake, Marc. You got a chance for a clean break."

Marc's head flopped to the right. "Yeah, yeah, that's true." He sighed heavily. "I don't know what to do. I . . . just don't . . . know."

"I'll tell you what you'll do," Harris said with a wise-acre grin. "You'll make a damn fool of yourself like every other lovesick guy and go crawling on the floor after her."

Marc squinted. And then he raised his hand toward the ceiling. "I will not crawl," he shouted so loudly that the rest of the bar patrons turned to look at him. Marc was oblivious to being the center of attention. "Do you hear me out there, Dr. Rusman, wherever you are? I will not crawl." He had to drop his hand and grab onto the bar to keep from toppling, but once he was moderately steady again, he smiled smugly at Harris Porter. "I will kneel on one knee, but I will not crawl."

John chuckled. "That's the way, Marc. Propose to Hannah in style."

Harris merely shook his head.

Marc lifted his already empty glass to his lips, gulped anyway and set it down, hiccupping. "Now all I have to do ish shee if I can get an appointment from her shecretary."

12

I Do. I Do.

439 Park Avenue

HANNAH WALKED DISPIRITEDLY into the apartment and flicked on the hall light. Shaking the snow from her coat, she hung it on a coat tree hook, noting with a sinking sensation that Marc's coat wasn't hung up, which meant he hadn't arrived home. It was close to 9:00 p.m.

They'd barely talked that morning. Marc had slept in *his* room, waking at the crack of dawn to pack for his L.A. trip. His flight wasn't until tomorrow, but he'd seemed bent on getting his things together ahead of time. He hadn't said whether he'd be home tonight, but then she hadn't asked. Nor had she asked what they should do about the apartment now that they weren't married. As painful as it was, Hannah thought a clean break was their best bet, even if she hadn't yet gotten up the courage to say it.

What a fool she'd been to think she and Marc could ever make a go of it. They hadn't had a marriage, they never had time for a marriage. So why, she wondered mordantly, if her career was so damn important to her, was she not the least bit excited about her upcoming London trip and the strong likelihood of the opportunity to head up a whole new branch of Unicom overseas? And she knew, if she'd told Marc about it, he wouldn't even have been resentful. He'd be happy for her, proud of her, supportive.

She walked into her bedroom and started getting undressed. In her slip, she sat down wearily on the bed. The queen-size bed built for two. Only she could count on her fingers the times the two of them had shared that bed for a whole night. They'd been so disgustingly considerate of each other that even on the nights they'd made love, Marc would more often than not shuffle off to his room to sleep so that he wouldn't disturb her in the morning when he got up early.

Hannah slipped on her robe and left the bedroom. After a brief hesitation in the hall, she wandered down to Marc's room. She wanted to see if his suitcase was still there. If it was, it would mean he'd be coming home before taking off for L.A. Tonight, she hoped. But there was the possibility he'd stop by for his case in the morning. Now that she'd given him his out by turning down his proposal to get married again, maybe he wanted to take his freedom and run for the nearest exit.

Marc's door was closed and Hannah could see her hand trembling as she reached for the knob. A rush of panic suffused her. If the suitcase was gone . . .

A gasp of utter despair escaped her lips as she finally took courage and opened the door to his room, and discovered that the suitcase was gone.

And so was everything else in the room. Everything. Marc's bed, his desk, file cabinets, computer equipment, bureaus. The closet was empty save for a few naked wire hangers.

Marc had moved out lock, stock and barrel. Without a word, a note, anything. Hannah felt a mix of such fury and sorrow the only thing she could think to do was throw something. But there wasn't a damn thing to throw. Except, she discovered by its ring, the telephone, which was lying on the floor behind the door.

She was going to let it go, let her machine take a message, but then she thought it might be Marc. She answered the phone on the fourth ring.

"Hello," she whispered nervously.

"Hannah? Is that you?"

"Oh. Mother."

"Did you just walk in? You sound a bit out of breath."

"Uh...yes. Yes, I just walked in." Hannah strived for a semblance of normalcy in her voice.

"Is Marc home yet?"

"Marc?" Even saying his name aloud hurt. She felt cold and miserable.

"Marc Welles? Your husband," Mary Logan said with a little laugh. "I know the two of you keep crazy schedules, but I thought you just might have possibly bumped into him lately."

"No. I mean...he's...in L.A."

There was a slight pause. "L.A.?"

Hannah sank down along the wall to the floor and closed her eyes, salty tears escaping her lids. "Business."

"Oh. I thought you told me the other day he wasn't leaving for L.A. until Thursday."

Hannah pressed her fingers against her temple. Her head had begun to pound. "He left...early." How she longed to just break down and tell her mother the whole sad tale. Hannah felt so alone and needy. How could Marc have thought she didn't have needs. She was a jangling mass of needs. *Oh, Mom, he's left me for good. I gave him an out and he grabbed it so fast it's all a blur to me. He's gone. I'm single. I'm free. I'm miserable.*

"Damn," Mary Logan muttered. "Simon's out of town for a couple of days, and he wanted me to find out more about this new navigational device for his boat that Marc had mentioned to him a while back."

"Navigational device? What does Marc know about that?"

"Why, Hannah, surely you know about the summer Marc spent crewing at a yachting club down in Newport, Rhode Island. The summer before he went on to Columbia for his business degree."

"He did? He . . . never said anything to me about it."

"Well, you ask him to tell you. Marc regaled Simon and I with any number of amusing stories about his experiences when he came over for dinner one night when you were out of town. The only thing funnier was his experience out in Minnesota being a caddie at the golf club. Marc is really quite a talented raconteur, Hannah. And neither of us could believe how wonderfully he played Simon's banjo. You never told me Marc was so talented musically."

"The banjo?" Hannah murmured weakly.

"Mean, hot Dixieland," Mary Logan said with a laugh. "I think it's a shame he doesn't spend more time doing the things he enjoys."

Hannah had no idea Marc had so many interests outside of work. She thought work was his whole life. She had no idea he could sail, or that he'd been a golf

caddie, or that he could play a mean hot banjo and re-
gale people with funny stories.

"I told him," Hannah's mother was saying, "that he
was to come over for a nice home-cooked meal more
often when you were working late or out of town. Of
course, I promised not to make eggplant again. You
never mentioned your husband was allergic to
eggplant."

Marc was allergic to eggplant? It was the last straw.
Hannah was beside herself. "Don't you think that's
something a husband should tell his wife? I mean,
Mother, don't you think if a husband is allergic to
eggplants, he . . . he owes it to his wife to tell her? What
if I'd gone and made eggplant, and . . . and pureed it so
he didn't know it was eggplant and . . . and he went and
ate it? What if he got ill from it? Or . . . or died? I suppose it would be my fault. I suppose I was supposed to
pause in my wedding vows and say to him, now Marc,
are you allergic to eggplant? And what about zuc-
chini? Or . . . or strawberries? Or radishes? Or . . ."

"Hannah, what are you going on about? Darling,
you have never cooked an eggplant in your life. To my
knowledge you have never pureed anything. You're
really acting very strangely, Hannah. I know you hate
when I say this, but I think you're working too hard. I
think you need a break. Marc, too. You know, the two
of you didn't have much of a honeymoon. It's very close
to your anniversary, Hannah. Why don't you and Marc
go off somewhere? I don't mean squeeze it between a
Tuesday and a Thursday. Take a couple of weeks. Take
a month. God, you've both worked hard enough and
long enough. You both deserve it. You both need it. It

would do wonders for you and Marc." She emitted a little laugh. "Tell Marc that Simon will even lend him his banjo so that he can serenade you."

It was the sorrowful thought that she would probably never hear Marc serenade her on a banjo that made her almost lose control and tell her mother the pathetic truth. But even as she was getting up the nerve to tell her, her mother had switched to a discussion of her upcoming wedding. There was such joy and excitement in her mother's voice, Hannah once again realized that she couldn't dump her own problems on her.

Instead Hannah said, "I am planning to go away for a while."

"Oh? On a vacation, you mean?"

"Well—business and . . . pleasure. To London." The only pleasure being a chance to get away from any painful reminders of Marc. Maybe in London she would forget. . . .

"For how long?" her mother asked.

"A month anyway. Maybe . . . longer."

There was a pause. "Marc's joining you, isn't he?"

"No, Mother. Unicorn is sending me to scout out an overseas branch."

"I see." There was clear disapproval and disappointment in Mary Logan's voice.

And, of course, she didn't see.

"I think it's for the best, Mother."

"I don't suppose you want my two cents?"

"No."

"Well, then all I'll say is I hope Marc has the good sense to talk you out of it."

After Hannah hung up, she gave Marc's empty room a sweeping look. And then she had herself a good cry, cursing Marc, and even more vehemently cursing poor Mrs. Sheldon. Hannah knew it wasn't fair to shoot the messenger of ill tidings, but if Mrs. Sheldon from City Hall hadn't come looking for that damn marriage certificate, she and Marc would still be . . .

Suddenly, like a woman possessed, Hannah darted from the room. Racing madly around the house, she began searching in earnest for the missing marriage certificate. Maybe it was pointless and dumb, and maybe she was only fooling herself, but if she could put her hands on that certificate she and Marc would still be officially married.

Okay, maybe Marc would still want out. But, it would be more complicated. It would require some discussion, communication. Communication. That would certainly be something new for them. Time to talk. Time to find out that Marc played a mean banjo and was allergic to eggplant. Time to share with him some of her likes and dislikes, display some of her talents. Did he know she could paint? Did he know she used to write poetry. Did he know she once won a table tennis championship at camp? Did he even know she was a Girl Scout with the most merit badges in her troop? No, he didn't know. Did he know she loved cotton candy? Did he know she hated seeded rye? No, he didn't know. Did he know that she wanted to have a baby? No, he didn't know. They'd never even talked about having children. Okay, so she'd never realized until now that she did want a baby. But, she did. She did. . . .

She pulled apart every drawer in her desk, pulled out every file in her file cabinet, went through her bureaus, her closets, the kitchen drawers, the entertainment center in the living room. There was no marriage certificate to be found.

Exhausted and miserable, she sank down on the sofa, trying to mentally recreate that day at City Hall. She closed her eyes and began to visualize the brief wedding ceremony. The visualization exercise was working. Dr. Rusman would have been proud of her. She even saw first Marc and then herself signing the certificate. Then she was able to picture the clerk sliding the certificate into the white envelope. And then . . .

Hannah's eyes sprang open. She remembered. She had taken the certificate and put it in her pocketbook. Her gray leather pocketbook with the cobra-skin trim. Hannah felt a sinking sensation in the pit of her stomach. The same bag she'd packed up with a pile of other items several weeks ago and given to her mother for one of the shelters for the homeless at which she did volunteer work.

Hannah rushed to the phone and dialed her mother. Maybe, just maybe, her mother hadn't given the collection to the shelter yet.

"Why, yes, Hannah. Weeks ago."

"Which shelter was it, Mother?" Maybe she could go down there. Someone might have spotted the certificate and handed it in to the office.

"I'm not really sure. I believe my collections were going to be sent down south. Georgia, I think. Well, it might have been Arkansas. I'm glad you asked about the donation though."

"Yes? You are?"

"Yes, I've got a tax receipt for you. I know how you and Marc like to do your taxes early. Is that why you were asking?"

Hannah sighed. "Yes, Mother, that's why."

Just as Hannah was hanging up the phone, she heard a key turn in the door.

Marc! He'd come back! Hannah pressed her hands to her flushed cheeks. After her scavenger hunt around the house for the marriage certificate, she looked a mess. She madly struggled to make order out of her disheveled appearance as she heard Marc's footsteps.

"Hey," he said, sauntering into the living room.

"Hey," Hannah whispered, swallowing hard.

"Did you eat yet?" he asked.

Hannah squinted. Her unofficial husband moves out of their apartment lock, stock and barrel, then casually saunters back and all he asks is, "Did you eat yet?" What did he expect? That she'd come home, found his room cleaned out and sat down and had herself a celebratory feast?

"No, I didn't eat," she snapped.

"Good," he said with a mysterious smile, turning and heading back to the front door.

"Okay, gentlemen," she heard him say at the door.

Baffled, Hannah pulled her robe more tightly closed just as two regal-looking white-coated waiters wheeled in a white linen-covered table on which there were several silver-domed platters. A third waiter, this one dressed in a black tux, followed, carrying a bottle of champagne, an ice bucket and a stand.

Speechless, Hannah watched Marc direct the men to a space in front of the fireplace. Two chairs were arranged at the table, the champagne was opened and placed in its bucket, and then Marc gave a signal and the three men silently departed.

Hannah stared at Marc. "What's going on?"

He walked over to the table and pulled out a chair for her. "Sit down, Hannah."

She came over and sat down. Instead of sitting down beside her, Marc turned and went back to the front door. Hannah wouldn't have been surprised to find the chef himself coming in to serve the meal.

But it wasn't the chef. It was a three-piece combo. Marc stationed them just inside the living-room entry, a discreet distance from the table. They started playing "Mood Indigo." It was Hannah's favorite. She didn't even know how Marc knew. She didn't think she'd ever told him.

As the musicians played, Marc lit the candles on the table, shut off all the lights, poured champagne into her crystal goblet and then into his, and sat down across from her.

Hannah stared at him, dazed. "You moved everything out. I . . . I thought . . . you'd gone."

He lifted his goblet and cradled it in both hands. "Do you remember that night on our honeymoon, Hannah?"

Hannah didn't have to ask which night he meant. "Yes," she murmured. "It was an unforgettable night."

"That night I felt whole, complete. Incredibly happy. Indescribably in love. I thought to myself, I have what I want at last." He kept cradling the goblet never bringing it to his lips. "We've made some really dumb mistakes, Hannah."

"Dumb, dumb, dumb," she whispered, unable to take her eyes off Marc, unable to stop thinking about how much she loved the way he looked, the sound of his voice, the warmth and sensuality in his eyes, his smile, his shiny white teeth. . . .

"We were so bent on doing everything right," Marc went on, "that we did everything wrong. We ended up being partners in a dummy company."

Hannah nodded her head.

"I don't want to go through that again," he said quietly.

It was hard to hear him say that to the strains of "Mood Indigo." "No," she said in a tight voice. "It wasn't much fun."

"No, it wasn't. It wasn't what I wanted, Hannah. And I'm ashamed to say I was too much of a coward to tell you it wasn't. I wanted a wife, not a limited partner."

"I . . . wanted a husband," Hannah admitted. "I wanted a husband I could talk to, lean on, play with, tell secrets to, discover new heights with. . . ."

"Your work was all-important. I didn't fit into your schedule in a neat, tidy way."

"You were no different," Hannah countered, the background music beginning to grate on her. "I put so much energy into my work because you were putting so much into yours. I thought you wanted a self-sufficient wife."

"I wanted a wife who spent more time respecting my hungers and desires for understanding and affection, and less time respecting my right to privacy."

Hannah glared at him. "Maybe if you'd had the decency to tell me. But, no, you never told me anything. Not about wanting more of my time and affection, not about the banjo, or eggplant or... or anything." She swung around to the trio who'd segued into, "I Don't Know Why I Love You Like I Do". "Will you all please shut up."

The music came to an abrupt stop and the trio shuffled from the living room into the hallway out of sight.

"Oh, that was nice, Hannah," Marc snapped. "I try to be a little romantic, create some atmosphere—"

"You created some atmosphere all right. You sure changed the look of your bedroom."

"And you don't even know why, do you?" He was shouting now.

"Oh, I know why, all right," Hannah shouted back. "Because as soon as I let you off the hook, you couldn't wait to clear out of here fast enough."

"That's what you think."

"That's what I think."

Marc leapt up from the table and grabbed her, pulling her up with him. "Well, you're wrong. I moved all that stuff out for one reason and one reason only."

"Okay, I'll play. What was the reason?" Hannah demanded.

"Because I love you, damn it. And I want to marry you," he shouted. He was grabbing her hard and he loosened his hold just a little. "I want to really marry you, Hannah," he said in a softer voice. "I want this apartment to be our real home. Not a dual work-station. I want one bedroom, one bed. Our bedroom, our bed. I want you to be the last person I talk to at night and the first person I greet the next morning. I want a real wife, Hannah. And I want to be a real husband. I want a reordering of our priorities. I want—"

"Hold it," Hannah said breathlessly. "What about what I want?"

"What you want is important, Hannah. What do you want?" He put his arms around her and they shared a giddy kiss. "Tell me what you want."

"I...want...a real wedding. A church wedding. With a to-die-for wedding gown, and bridesmaids, and a flower girl, even if she gets sick and throws up on my train."

He grinned. "Deal."

"And I want...a real honeymoon, not a couple of days squeezed into our work schedule."

"How about Paris? Three weeks in Paris?"

"Two weeks in Paris, one week in Venice."

"Deal."

"I want...to learn how to cook and then I want us both to make some of those favorite recipes of yours your mother gave me."

Marc shook his head. "Don't ever tell my mother, but she really wasn't such a hot cook. Let's discover new favorites together."

"Deal," she whispered with a sultry smile.

He touched her face gently. "Anything else?"

Her smile deepened. "One more thing that I can think of for right now."

He traced the outline of her lips with his index finger. "I know."

"You do?"

"Play something romantic," he called out to the musicians in the hallway. A moment later, music filled the room. Marc dropped down on one knee and took hold of Hannah's hand, sandwiching it between both of his. "Hannah, I love you desperately and I can't live without you. Will you marry me? Will you be my true and only wife for life?"

Tears glistened on Hannah's cheeks as she dropped down to her knees so that she and Marc could be face to face. "Yes, my darling. I'll marry you. And I'll try to be the best wife I can be."

They looked at each other in wonderment. As though getting married was something they had just miraculously invented. They touched lightly. They both shivered. And then they kissed, deeply, greedily, joyfully.

When she got her breath back, Hannah smiled. "That was nice, but it wasn't it. There's still something else I want."

He laughed, touching her hair, her face, her neck, as if he were inhaling her essence with his fingertips. "Whatever it is, it's yours."

"I want to open a joint bank account and I want it to say on top, Hannah Logan-Welles and Marc Welles...."

The two-hundred-dollar dinner for two sat congealing on the linen-covered table. The musicians had played their last tune and discreetly exited before Marc carried Hannah into their bedroom. Hannah and Marc lay contentedly entwined in each other's arms on their big queen-size bed.

The phone rang.

Hannah nuzzled her head against Marc's shoulder. "Let the machine pick it up."

The message was from her mother.

"Hannah, when you called earlier and asked about that bundle of yours for the shelter, I completely forgot to mention that you hadn't cleaned out a couple of the pocketbooks you had donated. There probably wasn't anything important in them, but I just wanted you to know I did collect everything and put it all in a manila envelope. You might want to check through it. Maybe there are some receipts or something you and Marc might need for your taxes. When you get the chance..."

A special gift for Christmas

Four romantic stories by four of your favourite
authors for you to unwrap and enjoy this
Christmas.

Robyn Donald   STORM OVER PARADISE
Catherine George   BRAZILIAN ENCHANTMENT
Emma Goldrick   SMUGGLER'S LOVE
Penny Jordan   SECOND-BEST HUSBAND

Published on 11th October, 1991   Price: £6.40

This month's irresistible novels from

—TEMPTATION—

A REBEL AT HEART by Gina Wilkins

Being confronted by ex-lover Griff Taylor was a real challenge for Melinda James. She knew that underneath the facade of silk ties and conservative haircuts lay a rebellious, untamed man . . . and a passionate lover. Could she make him betray himself?

DIFFERENT WORLDS by Elaine K. Stirling

One hot, steamy night in Costa Rica brought Dawn Avery and Michael Garrett together in a brief, passionate affair that left them aching for more. But they were worlds apart . . .

MAKING IT by Elise Title

For Hannah Logan marriage was just another business proposition. Marc Welles believed that sentiment and business didn't mix. So what were they doing getting married? It was obvious that their well-ordered lives were soon going to be turned upside-down.

DÉTENTE by Emma Jane Spenser

They were complete opposites and Kassidy and Matt should have known that their marriage was doomed. Soon they were leading separate lives until Matt realized that while marriage had been a mistake, living apart was worse. Making up was easy . . . but could they make it last?

Spoil yourself next month
with these four novels from

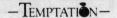
— TEMPTATION —

TOO WILD TO WED? by Jayne Ann Krentz

Xavier Augustine had had his fiancée investigated to
find out if she were perfect wife material. Letty Conroy
had led a scandal-free life, but she determined that this
impudent man would find something wild and naughty
about her . . .

TERMINALLY SINGLE by Kate Jenkins

Family tradition dictated that Ashley Atwood would
be the next maiden aunt, and no man had ever tempted
her to fight her fate. Then sexy Michael Jordan crossed
her path and set about finding the fire which lurked
beneath her button-tight exterior.

A MAN FOR THE NIGHT by Maggie Baker

Lust – not love – turned Susan Harkness into the
passionate woman who had dragged Nick Taurage to
bed on their first – and only – date. She had wanted to
impress her colleagues and Nick was the most in-
triguing man she had ever met, but he was *not* the man
for her.

THAT STUBBORN YANKEE by Carla Neggers

Harlan Rockwood's ex-wife was a woman to be
approached with caution. Hot-tempered, dangerously
beautiful, Beth had already once ordered him out of
her life. He couldn't decide whether the thugs who
were out to get him or hiding out with Beth would be
the more hazardous to his health.